Luigi Tansillo

The nurse

A poem

Luigi Tansillo

The nurse
A poem

ISBN/EAN: 9783337056674

Printed in Europe, USA, Canada, Australia, Japan

Cover: Foto ©Andreas Hilbeck / pixelio.de

More available books at **www.hansebooks.com**

THE NURSE.

THE

NURSE,

A

POEM.

TRANSLATED FROM THE ITALIAN

OF

LUIGI TANSILLO.

———————

BY WILLIAM ROSCOE.

———————

LIVERPOOL,

PRINTED BY J. M^cCREERY,

FOR CADELL AND DAVIES, STRAND,

LONDON.

1798.

LUIGI TANSILLO, the author of the following poem, was a native of Nola, a very ancient city of the kingdom of Naples and distinguished as a Roman colony. His family was of high rank and had been honoured by many public employments. In what year he was born is not with certainty known; but that event is conjectured, with great probability, to have taken place about the year 1510. The chief part of his life was spent in a military capacity, in the service of Don Piero di Toledo, Marquis of Villa-Franca, and Viceroy of Naples; and of Don Garzia his son, afterwards Viceroy of Sicily and Catalonia, under Philip the second; but the particulars of it have not been preserved to the present times so minutely as his merits seem to have required.— A poet and a soldier, he lived a long, and probably a diversified life; but although some incidents respecting it are of sufficient notoriety, the attempt to trace it through a regular narrative, would now be of no avail.

The result of this union of occupations in Tansillo, was exemplified in a want of due attention to his literary productions, few of which were published in his life time, and of the remainder scarcely any one received those advantages of revisal and correction, without which works of taste must always appear to disadvantage,

advantage. Notwithstanding these circumstances, his character as a poet stood high even among the most eminent of his contemporaries. In the dialogue of Torquato Tasso, entitled *Il Gonzago*, that celebrated author enumerates Tansillo amongst the few writers to whose sonnets he gives the appellation of *leggiadre*, or elegant. The same opinion has been confirmed by subsequent critics, cited by Zeno in his *Giornale d' Italia*, vol. xi. one of whom in particular has not hesitated to assert that Tansillo is a much better lyric poet than even Petrarca himself. It must however be observed, that this kind of commendation, which is intended to elevate one distinguished character at the expense of another, is of all praise the most equivocal. As every good author has his peculiar excellencies, so he will have his peculiar admirers. What purpose is answered by disputing whether the grape, the nectarine, or the pine apple, be the most exquisite fruit?

The first production by which Tansillo distinguished himself was a poem in *ottava rima*, which injured his moral character as much as it increased his reputation for talents and for wit. Perhaps no part of modern Europe has retained the customs of the ancients with so little variation as the kingdom of Naples, and particularly the provinces of Appulia and Calabria, where the most singular, and even obscene ceremonies are yet continued; the object in honour of whom they are performed being only changed from a heathen deity, to a modern saint. That liberty, or rather licentiousness of speech in which the Romans indulged their servants at a particular period of the year, and to which Horace adverts in the seventh satire of his second book, seems to have been transferred by the Neapolitans to a more cheerful season,

son, and their *Saturnalia* may be said to have been celebrated at the time of their vintage. At this time all respect to rank, to sex, and even to decency, seems to be entirely discarded, and the lowest of the peasantry, whilst engaged in the vintage, employ the most abusive and licentious language, not only to their fellow labourers, but to any persons who may happen to be present on this occasion. " At vero vindemiatores, ea die qua pro quo-
" quam vindemiam faciunt, atque per totum vindemiæ tempus,
" Baccho deo pleni esse, ac furere prorsus videntur. In agro
" quinetiam, in quo vindemiant, semper pudibunda vindemiando
" inclamant, obscænasque quisque partes suis nominibus pronun-
" ciantes, veneres vel obscœnissimas se optare exclamant. Mo-
" nentem vero si quis eos castigare velit, derident, ac exerta lin-
" gua contemnunt, oreque ipso in eum oppedunt : pudor nullus :
" reverentia omnis deleta est in eis : loquendi summa licentia at-
" que arrogantia in promptu est. Demum non homines videntur
" sed Satyri ac Bacchi sacerdotes, petulantes, injurii, lascivientes
" luxuriantes." Such is the portrait of his countrymen at this season given by Ambrogio Leone, an historian of Nola; but no sooner is the vintage completed, than these frantic Bacchanals are restored to their senses, and all their obscenity, folly, and abuse, is immediately forgotten. This extraordinary custom is the subject of the poem of Tansillo, to which he therefore gave the title of *Il Vendemmiatore,* and in which he introduces one of those extravagant characters addressing himself to his fellow labourers, not indeed with all the ribaldry which probably takes place on these occasions, but with much more freedom than a strict regard to decency will allow. The licentiousness of this piece was, it is true, in some degree concealed, if not compensated, by the wit and delicate humour with which it abounds; for, as a late noble
author

author has justly observed, " indecency is far from conferring wit, but it does not destroy it neither." But the admiration which it excited did not prevent its producing a most unfavourable effect on the fortunes of the author, who seems during the remainder of his days severely to have felt the consequences of his early imprudence, and to have endeavoured to make amends for it by a more regulated conduct and by more serious labours.

This poem was written whilst the author was attending the vintage in the year 1534, and when he was consequently about twenty-four years of age. On the first of October, in that year, he sent a copy of it to his friend Caraffa, at Naples, intreating him not to make it public, but to suffer it to perish by the moths in a gradual and natural decay. " Because," says he, " it would be " too severe and cruel an act to destroy my own offspring, " however base-born and illegitimate it may be." Notwithstanding this injunction, it made its appearance in the same year at Naples, in a small quarto of eight leaves, under the before mentioned title, and was afterwards printed with many variations, in several collections of Italian poetry. The obscene *Stanze in lode della Menta*, have also been attributed to Tansillo, and bear so strong a resemblance to his manner, that they have in some editions been united with, and form a part of the *Vendemmiatore*.

In the year 1539, Tansillo accompanied his great benefactor Don Garzia di Toledo, then general of the Neapolitan galleys to Sicily, where, in the month of December in the same year, that nobleman gave a splendid reception to Donna Antonia Cardona, daughter of the Marquis of Collesano, to whom he then paid his addresses. On this occasion Tansillo wrote a pastoral comedy, which

which was performed with the greatest degree of splendor and expense. The stage made use of for this purpose was raised upon the water, and consisted of three large gallies, which were placed at regular distances, so as nearly to adjoin the gardens of the palace, and over which a platform was laid, extending to the shore; the whole was then covered with canvas, and lined with exquisite tapestry, representing, like the palace of Dido, the most remarkable circumstances of the Trojan war. From the description given of the representation of this piece, Fontanini conjectures, that Tansillo is entitled to the honour of being the first Italian who set the example of the pastoral comedy which was afterwards brought to perfection by Tasso and Guarini, but in this, as in many other particulars respecting Italian literature, he is mistaken; for it is certain that the first idea of this elegant species of comedy was given by Politiano in the preceding century in his dramatic fable entitled *Orfeo*.

However unfavourable may be the inferences against the morals and manners of Tansillo, arising from his early works, it is no less certain that his life was honourable and his conduct irreproachable; but in the year 1559, all his writings, which at that time consisted only of the *Vendemmiatore*, and a few lyric productions, were inserted by Pius IV. in the *Index Expurgatorius*, under the title of *Aloysii Tansilli Carmina*; a circumstance which appears to have given him no small degree of concern. For some time prior to this event he had employed his leisure on a poem of considerable extent, entitled *Le lagrime di San Piero*—THE TEARS OF ST. PETER.; which subject it is highly probable he chose in allusion to his regret in having been the author of the *Vendemmiatore*. Not however having brought it to a termination
when

when this weighty sentence was passed upon his works, he addressed an ode to the Pope, in which he endeavours, by the humblest submission, and the most respectful entreaties, to induce him to remove the censures under which he laboured, asserting, that the tenor of his life had never been injured by the levity of his writings.

Fu, gran Padre, la carta,
Vana talor, la vita sempre onesta,
E tal sarà quanto di lei mi resta.

Chaste was my life, tho' wanton was my page,
Nor shall one blot deform my riper age.

This, it is true, has been the apology of all licentious authors from the days of Catullus, but with respect to Tansillo, it is to be regarded, as Zeno admits, not as a poetical fiction, but as the dictates of truth. The language in which he proceeds to condemn the verses of his youth, are peculiarly strong and impressive.

Peccai, me stesso accuso, a Dio rivolte,
Ho lingua e mano; ambedue tronche & secche,
Vorrei piùtosto, ch' esser qual già fui
Cagion talor d'obliqui essempj altrui.

I own my fault—in youthful years unaw'd
My hands—my tongue—were rais'd against my God.
Sever'd, or shrivell'd, may they hide my crimes,
Ere my example injure future times.

He fails not however to make a just and pointed distinction between his *Vendemmiatore* and his other writings; contending, that although

although divine and human laws often punish the children for the crimes of the parent, it had never been usual to extend the punishment due to the guilty to all his innocent brethren. He then adverts to his poem on the tears of St. Piero, expressing his hopes that it will not only compensate for his early writings, but obtain him true honour and reputation. The effect produced on the mind of the Pope by this pathetic address, exceeded even the hopes of the author, and in the next publication of the Index, not only the works of Tansillo were omitted, but even the poem of the *Vendemmiatore* was not to be found.

In the year 1551 Tansillo accompanied his great patron Don Garzia, on a successful expedition against the coast of Barbary, in which Don Garzia, under the auspices of Charles V. had the command of the Spanish fleet, and captured the city anciently called Aphrodisium. His associate, as well in his dangers, as in his amusements, Tansillo enjoyed the highest favour of this distinguished commander, who boasted, that he had in his service a Homer and an Achilles united in the same person; and Tansillo has more than recompensed his favour by the honourable mention which he has made of his patron in different parts of his works.

Of all the productions of Tansillo, the most estimable, as well in respect of the subject, as of the manner of execution, are his poems entitled *La Balia*, or The Nurse, and *Il Podere*, or The Country House; in the latter of which he gives directions for making a proper choice of a country residence, enlivening the barrenness of his subject with the happiest illustrations, and the most sportive wit. These poems, after the death of their author, were long neglected, although several persons have, at
different

different times, given indications of their existence. In particular the Venetian printer Barezzo Barezzi, who published in the year 1600 an edition of the *Lagrime di San Piero*, which is the best edition now extant, promised in his advertisement prefixed to that work, to give the public some beautiful *Capitoli* of the same author; which expression it is supposed could only relate to these poems, the former of which consists of two, and the latter of three capitoli, or cantos. Zeno also informs us, that many of the compositions of Tansillo undoubtedly lay buried in the Italian libraries, and adverts to a few of his poems, which had not then been in print.

In the year 1767, about two centuries after the death of the author, Giovan Antonio Ranza, regius professor of polite literature at Vercelli, had the good fortune to meet with a MS. copy of these two poems, accompanied with the *Vendemmiatore*, and the *Stanze in lode della Menta*, from which he gave to the public the first edition of the *Balia*, accompanied with many learned annotations. At the same time he informs us, that he had also written notes on the *Podere*, which would make its appearance in a few months, the reception of which he hoped would not be less favourable than that of the *Balia*. From some circumstances this promise was not fulfilled, and the *Podere* was not published, till the year 1770, when it was printed at Turin by Bonaventura Porro, to whom Ranza had conceded the MS. though without his notes; and was published by Zatta at Venice. An anonymous editor has, however enriched this edition by citing the passages from the ancient authors, which Tansillo has frequently imitated, in which he professes his intention to second the views of the author, who in a letter written in the

year

year 1566, to Antonio Scarampi, bishop of Nola, accompanying the two poems of the *Balia,* and the *Podere,* thus expresses himself, " You may now judge for yourself, whether I have known how " to distinguish the properties of a good soil, to erect my villa, " and to avail myself of the Mantuan bard, and of other writers."

That Tansillo had entered into the married state, and had superadded to the relation of a husband, that of a father, are circumstances only known from the ensuing poem. The time of his death is not less uncertain than that of his birth. Tiraboschi places this event in 1596, but Zeno conjectures it to have happened in the year 1569, whilst he was governor of Gaeta. At least in that year it is certain that he received as his guest Scipio Ammirato, then on his way to Florence, who relates in his *Opusculi,* that Tansillo being much indisposed and advanced in years, did not survive that event many months, nor had Zeno discovered any documents which tended to shew that the life of Tansillo had been extended beyond that year. It is however probable that some error has arisen either in the time assigned by Zeno to his birth, or in that of his death, as a person at the age of fifty-nine, can scarcely be considered as having reached a very advanced period of life.

With respect to the poem, of which an English translation is now attempted, it may certainly be considered as a singular and interesting production. As the work of one of the brightest wits in that constellation of Genius which appeared in Italy in the
sixteenth

sixteenth century, and which yet diffuses a permanent light over
the horizon of literature, it is worth notice and consideration.
Contemporary with Ariosto, with Bembo, with Casa, and with the
two Tassos, Tansillo was not perhaps inferior to any writer of
his time in the simplicity of his diction, the elegance of his taste,
or a strict adherence to nature and to truth. But independent of
the merit which the poem may be presumed to possess from the
acknowledged character of the author, it will be found on exami-
nation to contain within itself sufficient claims to the approbation
of the admirers of Italian poetry. The subject is in a high degree
interesting, and is treated in a manner peculiarly pointed and
direct, yet without violating that decorum which is due to the
public at large, and in particular to the sex to whom it is addressed. To those who feel the laudable curiosity, and ac-
knowledge the utility of comparing the manners of different ages,
it will afford many striking indications of the state of society at
the period in which it was written, and will tend to shew, that
the ideas and feelings of mankind on all subjects of general concern, are much less liable to variation from the diversity of time
and place, than is frequently supposed. Such is the coincidence
between the state of manners in Italy in the sixteenth century,
and in England in the eighteenth, that the translator, though in-
tending to accommodate the poem to modern times, has seldom
found it expedient to vary from the original in the slightest degree, and if he has not wholly failed in his purpose, he thinks it
will appear that it would be difficult even in the present day to
adduce arguments more pointedly directed than those of the author against the abuse which it was his purpose to reform.

It

It is not the translator's intention to assert, that a previous consideration of these circumstances led him to undertake the present version of the poem. The truth is, that having of late enjoyed a greater share of leisure than he has formerly experienced, he has employed some part of it pleasantly to himself, if not usefully to others, in an occupation, which without requiring the exertion of original composition, satisfies the *besoin d' agir*, and by calming the reproaches, allays the irritation of total indolence. He must also be allowed to observe, that the hope of promoting in some degree the laudable object which the author himself had in view, if it did not lead him to undertake the translation, operated as a chief inducement to lay it before the public. That the character and manners of our countrymen, both in higher and lower life, affords but too much room for reform, is an assertion which may be made without incurring the imputation of moroseness; but till we can decidedly point out those circumstances which give rise to this laxity, not to say depravity of manners of the present day, it will be to no purpose to adopt measures for their improvement. Of these causes the custom, still so prevalent, of committing the children of the richer and middle ranks of society to be brought up by the poor, is, in the opinion of the translator, one of the most efficacious, and like all other vicious institutions, its effects are injurious to all the parties who engage in it. The reason generally assigned by medical men for promoting a custom which has of late received their almost universal sanction, is, that the mode of living which now prevails in the higher ranks, is such, as renders it impossible for a woman to afford her infant those advantages which are indispensably necessary to its existence and support. But is it possible to conceive a severer satire
against

against the female sex than this assertion implies ? Such it seems is the rage for pleasure and amusement, that it must be gratified even by the sacrifice of the most important duties of life, and by a practice, which if generally extended, would endanger the very existence of the human race. The assistance of a nurse is not then intended as a benefit to the child, but as a licence to the mother to pursue her gratifications, without those restraints which the performance of her own proper and indispensible duties would impose upon her, and by the due exercise of which she would find her health and her affections equally improved. To trace the consequences of this practice further, would here be unnecessary, as they will be found adverted to in the ensuing poem, which, if it should produce in any degree the effect which its author intended, will be a much better compensation to mankind, for the indiscretions of his youthful pen, than even his poem on the *Lagrime di San Piero.*

The translator has only further to observe, that for the greater part of the authorities and quotations referred to in the notes, he is indebted to the Italian editor Ranza, the few additional observations which accompany them, are too unimportant to require an apology.

SONNET.

TO MRS. R.

AS thus in calm domestic leisure blest,
I wake to BRITISH *notes th'* AUSONIAN *strings,*
Be thine the strain ; for what the poet sings
Has the chaste tenor of thy life exprest.
And whilst delighted, to thy willing breast,
With rosy lip thy smiling infant clings,
Pleas'd I reflect, that from those healthful springs
—Ah not by thee with niggard love represt—
Six sons successive, and thy later care,
Two daughters fair have drank ; for this be thine
Those best delights approving conscience knows,
And whilst thy days with cloudless suns decline,
May filial love thy evening couch prepare,
And sooth thy latest hours to soft repose.

W. R.

LA BALIA.

CAPITOLO PRIMO.

DONNE ben nate, i cui bei colli preme
 Quel santissimo giogo d' Imeneo,
 Onde buon frutto spera ogni uman seme;

Se già mai voce io desiai d' Orfeo,
 (Com' uom che in cor di fera pietà brami)
 Mentre prigion di donna Amor mi feo;

Oggi, bench' io sia fuor di quei legami,
 Più che mai desiarla mi bisogna:
 Ch' esser, Donne, non può, ch' io pur non ami.

Amo, ma d' uno amor, che non agogna
 Cosa di reo; nè m' arde di desìo
 Che porti pentimento, nè vergogna.

THE NURSE.

CANTO I.

A<small>CCOMPLISH</small>'<small>D</small> D<small>AMES</small>, whose soft consenting minds
The rosy chain of willing Hymen binds!
If e'er one prouder wish my bosom felt
By magic strains the listening soul to melt,
(Mov'd by such strains the woodlands Orpheus drew,)
That wish inspires me whilst I sing to you.
—What tho' the pleasing bonds no more I prove,
I own your charms, nor e'er shall cease to love;
Not with such love as feeds a wanton flame,
—Attended close by penitence and shame!

But

D' Orfeo vorrei, che fosse ora il dir mio,
    Non perchè l'alma oppressa si rileve;
    Ma per darvi a veder quel, ch' io desìo.

Pur, se 'l vero ha la forza, ch' aver deve
    Negli animi gentili, come 'l vostro,
    Darlo a creder a voi mi sarà lieve.

Ne per desìo d' onor verso l' inchiostro,
    Ma per un zelo santo, e naturale,
    Che mi muove a pietà dell' error nostro;

E so, che l' emendar d' un sì gran male,
    O Donne, è in mano a voi, qualor vogliate;
    Se d' adoprar virtù punto vi cale.

Vero è, che questo error fu in ogni etate;
    Ma in nessuna già mai, quant' ora in questa;
    Onde maggior ne nasce la pietate.

Qual furia dell' inferno all' uom più infesta
    Addusse al mondo, e tanto crescer fece
    Usanza così fiera, e disonesta?

Che porti Donna nove mesi, o diece
    In ventre il parto; e poichè a luce è tratto,
    Lo schifi, ed altra prendalo in sua vece.

Quando io penso a sì crudo, orribil atto;
    E che dai più miglior più s' abbia in uso,
    Ne son per divenir rabbioso, o matto.

But Love, that seeks by nobler arts to please,
True to your honour, happiness and ease.

   Light were my task, if every gentle breast
Own'd the just laws of native truth imprest;
For not by hopes of vain applause misled,
In reason's injur'd cause alone I plead.
'Tis yours to judge ; nor I that judgment fear,
If truth be sacred and if virtue dear.

   What fury, hostile to our common kind,
First led from nature's path the female mind,
Th' ingenuous sense by fashion's laws represt,
And to a babe denied its mother's breast ?
What ! could she, as her own existence dear,
Nine tedious months her tender burthen bear,
Yet when at length it smil'd upon the day,
To hireling hands its helpless frame convey ?
—Whilst yet conceal'd in life's primæval folds,
Th' unconscious mass her proper body holds ; (a)
                   Whilst

Che mentr' ella nel corpo tenea chiuso
  Un non so che, che non vedea s' egli era
  Umor corrotto, o vento ivi rinchiuso;

O mola informe, o come dicon fera,
  Che talor sembri pipistrello, od angue;
  E toccando il terren, la donna pera;

Ella il nudrisce del suo proprio sangue,
  E'l guarda d' ogni mal, d' ogni periglio,
  E grave il ventre tanti dì ne langue:

E poi c' ha nelle braccia il caro figlio,
  Ella neghi notrirlo del suo latte;
  E talor quasi mandilo in esiglio:

Che quando nol vedea, gli abbia ella fatte
  Tante accoglienze; ed or che'l vede, e sente,
  Lo spregi, e sdegni, e sì vilmente il tratte:

Che'l veda nella cuna uom già vivente,
  E col bel pianto, e con la voce umana
  Quasi gridar mercè l' oda sovente:

E'l cibo usato suo, la sua fontana
  Non pur gli neghi, ma di casa il cacci;
  E' cosa troppo fiera, ed inumana.

Che al proprio figlio il petto altrui procacci,
  E'l suo gli chiuda, e mandilo in disparte;
  Par, che'n pensarvi il sangue mi si agghiacci.

THE NURSE.

Whilst in her mind distracting fears arise,
Stranger to that which in her bosom lies ;
Whilst led by ignorance, wild fancy apes
Uncouth distortions and perverted shapes ;
Yet then securely rests the promis'd brood,
Screen'd by her cares and nurtur'd by her blood.
But when reliev'd from danger and alarms,
The perfect offspring leaps into her arms,
Turns to a mother's face its asking eyes,
And begs for pity by its tender cries ;
Then, whilst young life its opening powers expands,
And the meek infant spreads its searching hands,
Scents the pure milk-drops as they slow distill,
And thence anticipates the plenteous rill,
From her first grasp the smiling babe she flings,
Whilst pride and folly scal the gushing springs ;
Hopeful that pity can by her be shewn,
Who for another's offspring quits her own.

Ah !

Come per mezzo il cor non se le parte,
    Quando in man d'una, che 'l suo sangue venda,
    Pon madre il figlio, e di suo grembo il parte?

Forse credete, che natura appenda
    Due poma al vostro petto, come al mento
    Suol porsi un neo, ch' ivi qual gemma splenda?

E che non le vi dia per nodrimento
    De' pargoletti figli, e per aita;
    Ma per beltà del corpo, ed ornamento?

Onde ciascuna appena in salvo uscita,
    Quel candido liquor scaccia, ed arretra;
    E non senza periglio di sua vita:

Mentre di bianco umor vien marcia tetra,
    E si spande nei membri, o giù sen cala;
    O dentro i vasi suoi gela, ed impetra.

Sbandite il latte come cosa mala,
    Che la vostra beltà denigri, o guaste;
    Onde più d'una l' animo n' esala.

Siate, Donne, quantunque e sante, e caste,
    Tra voi non ne trovo una oggi sì forte,
    Che incontro uso sì reo pugni, e contraste.

Lasso! La mia carissima consorte
    Sei mesi inferma io piansi sovra un anno,
    E sette volte quasi giunta a morte.

Ah! sure ye deem that nature gave in vain
Those swelling orbs that life's warm streams contain;
As the soft simper, or the dimple sleek
Hangs on the lip, or wantons in the cheek; (*b*)
Nor heed the duties that to these belong,
The dear nutrition of your helpless young.
—Why else, ere health's returning lustre glows,
Check ye the milky fountain as it flows?
Turn to a stagnant mass the circling flood,
And with disease contaminate the blood? (*c*)
Whilst scarcely one, however chaste she prove,
Faithful remains to nature and to love.

Nor think your poet feigns; alas too well
By dear experience I the truth can tell:
In dread suspense a year's long circuit kept,
And seven sad months, I trembled and I wept,
Whilst a lov'd consort press'd the couch of woe,
And death oft aim'd the oft averted blow.

Nor

Ma del suo mal fu mia la colpa, e 'l danno,
    Chè contro il suo voler deliberai,
    Che facess' ella quel, che l'altre fanno.

Se argento, ed oro, e lagrime versai,
    Ch' ogni gran vena sarìa spenta, e secca;
    Pensar sel può chi 'l prova, o 'l provò mai.

O quanto, Donne, gravemente pecca
    Colei, che con liquori, od erba, o polve
    Quelle fonti santissime dissecca !

Dissecca quelle fonti, o indietro volve,
    Che Dio diede all' età dell' innocenza,
    Mentre che nelle fasce ella s' involve.

Per me non credo, ch' abbia differenza
    Dall' un peccato all' altro, che gravi oncia;
    Ma sian quasi di pari penitenza,

Donna che pregna di sua man si sconcia,
    Perchè 'l ventre già molle non arrughi,
    Onde nuda talor ne paja sconcia;

Od altra, che del petto i rivi asciughi
    Per serbar tonde, e sode le sue poppe;
    E quel dono di Dio dal mondo fughi.

Quella d' uom cominciato il filo roppe,
    E qual ombra, che 'l seme in erba adugge,
    L' opra in man di natura ella interroppe :

—Nor her's the fault—misled by fashion's song,

'Twas I depriv'd the mother of her young ;

Mine was the blame, and I too shar'd the smart,

Drain'd was my purse, and anguish wrung my heart.

O crime ! with herbs and drugs of essence high,

The sacred fountains of the breast to dry !

Pour back on nature's self the balmy tide

Which Nature's God for infancy supplied !

—Does horror shake us when the pregnant dame,

To spare her beauties, or to hide her shame,

Destroys, with impious rage and arts accurst,

Her growing offspring ere to life it burst,

And can we bear, on every slight pretence,

The kindred guilt that marks this dread offence ? (d)

—As the green herb fresh from its earliest root

Young life protrudes its yet uncertain shoot,

Or falls, unconscious of the blighting storm,

A dubious victim, and a shadowy form ;

But

Questa, il cui parto il sangue suo non sugge,
  Offende uom già perfetto, uom giunto a luce ;
  E l' opra fatta, in quanto a sè distrugge.

A tor quel vitto al figlio empia s' induce,
  Ch' è suo, da che nel cor l' anima gli entre ;
  E ch' egli, uscendo fuor, seco s'adduce.

Forse quel sangue, già vermiglio mentre
  Giù si giacea, non è quel medesmo oggi
  Dentro le poppe, ch' era pria nel ventre ?

Il qual per dare all' uom, poi ch' indi sloggi,
  Senza schifo l' usato suo sostegno,
  Vuol Dio, che color muti, e su sen poggi.

Volete voi veder, se 'l suo disegno
  Nel far del mondo fu, che tra' mortali
  Ogni madre allattasse il caro pegno ?

Chè a tante, e tante guise d' animali,
  Fin a que' tanti mostri d' Etiopia
  Diede lor poppe, e non a tutti eguali.

Ne die' a voi due, non già per maggior copia ;
  Ma che accadendo far proli gemelle,
  Ciascun' avesse la sua fonte propia.

A cagne, a capre, a scrofe, a tutte quelle,
  Che son vie più feconde, ne die' molte ;
  Chè a par de' figli avesser le mammelle.

But she who to her babe her breast denies,
The sentient mind, the living man destroys;
Arrests kind nature's liberal hand too soon,
And robs her helpless young of half the boon. (*e*)
—'Tis his, not hers—the colour only chang'd,
Erewhile thro' all the throbbing veins it rang'd;
Pour'd thro' each artery its redundant tide,
And with rich stream incipient life supplied;
And when full time releas'd the imprison'd young,
Up to the breasts, a living river, sprung. (*f*)

Doubt ye the laws by Nature's God ordain'd,
Or that the callous young should be sustain'd
Upon the parent breast?—be those your schools
Where nature triumphs, and where instinct rules.
No beast so fierce from Zembla's northern strand,
To Ethiopia's barren realms of sand,
But midst her young her milky fountain shares,
With teats as numerous as the brood she rears.

Two

Può esser, care Donne, ch' alle volte
　Il core un verme non vi morda, e roda,
　Quando a pensar di voi siete rivolte?

Deh se bramate in terra e premio, e loda,
　Non siate, Donne, sì crudeli, ed empie,
　Facendo al mondo, ai vostri, ed a Dio froda.

Anzi ognuna di voi, prego, contempie
　Con quant' arte natura in voi governe,
　Quando del bel liquor le mamme v' empie :

Che, poi che nelle parti vie più interne
　Formò quel sangue, e fece di sè stesso
　Tutto il corpo dell' uom, qual fuor si scerne ;

E che 'l tempo del parto ne vien presso,
　Ei ne' luoghi di sopra se ne saglia ;
　E 'l cibo usato appresti all' uscir d' esso ;

E qual buon Capitan di vettovaglia
　Provveda alle sue genti d' ora in ora,
　Chè non teman di fame, che le assaglia :

E per diverse vie tutti in un' ora
　Quasi di pari passo camminando,
　Il parto, e 'l nutrimento vengan fora.

Or chi sarà colei, che contemplando
　In ciò l' affetto ardente di natura,
　Da sè non metta l' amor proprio in bando?

Two breasts ye boast for this kind end alone,
That your twin offspring each should have its own.

Does no remorse, ye fair, your bosoms gnaw,
Rebellious to affection's primal law ?
Persist ye still, by her mild voice unaw'd,
False to yourselves, your offspring, and your God ?
Mark but your proper frame—what wond'rous art,
What fine arrangement rules in every part ;
As the blood rushes thro' each swelling vein,
The ruddy tide appropriate vessels strain ;
And whilst around the limpid current flows,
To shape and strength th' unconscious embryon grows,
But when 'tis born, then nature's secret force
Gives to the circling stream another course ;
The starting beverage meets the thirsty lip,
'Tis joy to yield it, and 'tis joy to sip.
So when th' experienced chieftain leads along
To distant enterprize his warrior throng,

He,

E che non si disponga a soffrir dura
   Ed aspra vita, per nodrir suo parto
   Con ogni tenerezza, ed ogni cura?

Io non vo' dir, che'l popol Moro, e'l Parto
   Han le mogli di voi via più amorose;
   Ed ogni gente esposta all' Austro, all' Arto:

Ma per farvi vermiglie ambe le rose
   De' bei volti, dirovvi, Donne mie,
   Che son le fiere più di voi pietose.

Vi basta dunque il cor sendo sì pie,
   D' usar coi figli vostri la fierezza,
   Che non usan coi lor fiere più rie?

Venga qual sia più a carne umana avvezza,
   E lupa, e tigre ircana, e leoparda;
   Che ognuna i figli nutre, ed accarrezza.

Nè mai fiera è sì brava, e sì gagliarda,
   Come al tempo, ch' ella ha suoi figliuolini,
   E che gelosa se gli allatta, e guarda.

E' lupa, ch' avrà dieci lupicini,
   E tutti in seno se gli tiene stretti,
   Finchè ciascun per sè furi, e cammini.

Latte non han gli augelli ne' lor petti;
   Ma i vostri, o Donne, ben dovria far molli
   Il veder loro, e i figli pargoletti,

He, as they move, with ever watchful cares
Their stores of needful nutriment prepares ;
Still prompt, e'er hunger ask, or thirst invade,
With due supplies and stationary aid.

And can ye then, whilst nature's voice divine
Prescribes your duty, to yourselves confine
Your pleas'd attention ? Can ye hope to prove
More bliss from selfish joys than social love ?
Nor deign a mother's best delights to share,
Tho' purchas'd oft with watchfulness and care ?
—Pursue your course, nor deem it to your shame
That the swart African, or Parthian dame,
In her bare breast a softer heart infolds
Than your gay robe and cultur'd bosom holds ;
Yet hear, and blush, whilst I the truth disclose ;
Than you the ravening beast more pity knows.
Not the wild tenant of th' Hyrcanian wood,
Intent on slaughter, and athirst for blood,
E'er turns regardless from her offspring's cries,
Or to their thirst the plenteous rill denies.

Gaunt

Come sempre li tengono satolli :
  Io so, che avete nei poderi vostri,
  De' colombi, e dell' anatre, e de' polli :

Vedete i figli lor cibar coi rostri,
  Coprir con l'ale, e radunar col grido ;
  E in quanti modi l' amor lor si mostri.

Che fanno i cigni, da che son nel nido
  I nudi figli, sin che veston piume,
  Sì che possan volar di là dal lido ?

La madre sì li guarda, mentre il lume
  Ella ha del dì ; la notte il padre a nuoto
  Su l'ale li diporta per lo fiume.

So, che per fama quell' augel v' è noto,
  (Sebben non fè mai per nostr' aria il volo.)
  Ch' apre il suo petto ai figli sì devoto.

Fiere, ed augei nutron di figli un stuolo ;
  E voi, Donne gentil, Donne sovrane,
  Vi disdegnate di nodrirne un solo ?

Non pur le proprie carni, ma le strane
  Allevan bruti : è amicizia quella,
  O sdegno, ed odio, ch' è tra 'l gatto, e 'l cane ?

Gaunt is the wolf, the tyger fierce and strong,
Yet when the safety of their helpless young
Alarms their fears, the deathful war they wage
With strength unconquer'd, and resistless rage. (g)
One lovely babe your fostering care demands,
And can ye trust it to an hireling's hands?
Whilst ten young wolvelings shelter find and rest
In the soft precincts of their mother's breast ;
'Till forth they rush, with vigorous nurture bold,
Scourge of the plain, and terror of the fold.

Mark too the feather'd tenants of the air ;
What tho' their breasts no milky fountain bear,
Yet well may yours a soft emotion prove
From their example of maternal love.
On rapid wing the anxious parent flies
To bring her helpless brood their due supplies.
See the young pigeon from the parent beak
With struggling eagerness its nurture take.
The hen, whene'er the long sought grain is found,
Calls, with assiduous voice, her young around,

Then

E vist' ho in casa d' una mia sorella,
  Cagna morir, mentre i suoi figli allatta,
  Che viver non potean senza mammella ;

E nel suo loco entrar pietosa gatta,
  E nodrirgli, e crear fino all' etade
  Per sè stessa a cibarsi, e viver atta.

Nutre bestia i nemici per pietade ;
  E noi mandiamo i nostri figli altrove ?
  O vituperio dell' umanitade !

Di Spagna, dal Perù, dall' Indie nuove
  Recar vi fate or cagnin rosso, or bianco,
  E d' ogni estremo lido, in che si trove ;

E non vi si allontana mai dal fianco ;
  Non pur gli aprite il sen, gli date il lembo ;
  Ma in petto a fiato a fiato il chiudete anco.

E i figli vostri, che nè sol, nè nembo
  Dovria scostar da voi, par che vi grave
  Tener ne' tetti ; io non vo' dir nel grembo ?

Senza che di sua mano asterga, e lave,
  Nodrir può figlio gentil Donna accorta,
  Onde poi maggior debito se n' ave.

Then to her breast the little stragglers brings,

And screens from danger by her guardian wings.

Safe thro' the day beneath a mother's eye,

In their warm nest the unfledg'd cygnets lie ;

But when the sun withdraws his garish beam,

A father's wing supports them down the stream.

—Yet still more wonderous (if the long told tale

Hide not some moral truth in fiction's veil)

The Pelican her proper bosom tears,

And with her blood her numerous offspring rears,

Whilst you the balmy tide of life restrain,

And truth may plead, and fiction court in vain.

Yon favorite lap-dog that your steps attends,

Peru, or Spain, or either India sends.(*h*)

What fears ye feel, as slow ye take your way,

Lest from its path the minion chance to stray !

At home on cushions pillow'd deep he lies,

And silken slumbers veil his wakeful eyes ;

Or still more favoured, on your snowy breast

He drinks your fragrant breath, and sinks to rest ;

Whilst

Di nulla figlio a Madre obbligo porta ;
　Come quando ella stessa sel notrica ;
　Sebben giacque per lui più volte morta.

Il generarlo vien senza fatica.

　　*　　　*　　　*

　　*　　　*　　　*

Il girne grave è atto necessario,
　La tema, il rischio, il partorir, la doglia ;
　Solo il tenerlo a petto è volontario.

Ma che Donna non possa, o che non voglia
　Nutrir suo parto ; almen più destro modo
　S' usasse in cercar femmina, che'l toglia.

Ove che sia, per quanto io veggo, ed odo,
　Quel che più nelle Balie si domanda,
　È il latte fresco, e 'l petto colmo, e sodo :

E si prende ugualmente, e d' ogni banda,
　Ove si trovi ; e spesso a prender viensi
　Per un vil servitor, che a ciò si manda.

E s' ella è putta, o rea ; se ha scemi sensi,
　O s' altro ell' ha di mal, quando si piglia,
　Nessuno è che vi miri, o che vi pensi :

Whilst your young babe, that from its mother's side
No threats should sever, and no force divide,
In hapless hour is banish'd far aloof
Not only from your breast—but from your roof.

Think not that I would bid your softness share
Undue fatigue, and every grosser care,
Another's toils may here supply your own,
But be the task of nurture yours alone ;
Nor from a stranger let your offspring prove
The fond endearments of a parent's love.
So shall your child, in manhood's riper day,
With warm affection all your cares repay.
But if the milk-stream on his lips you close
No other debt your injur'd offspring owes ;(i)
You gave him life, as powerful impulse taught,
The fated months roll'd onward, till they brought
The hour of dread, of danger, and of pain,
That hour you sought to deprecate in vain ;
Spontaneous then supply the milky spring ;
The only voluntary boon ye bring.

But

S' è bianca, o bruna, o pallida, o vermiglia ;
  E 'n complession (che ben si mostra al viso)
  È contraria alla madre, o le somiglia.

Ed è questo un accorto, util avviso
  D' importanza quant' altro, ch' io ne scorga,
  Prima che 'l figlio sia da voi diviso.

Purchè, qual pianta, il fanciullin ne sorga ;
  Che importa, alcun dirà, chi sia la donna,
  Che in grembo il cresca, e 'l petto suo gli porga ?

Sieno avi del fanciullo Orso, e Colonna ;
  E sia la Balia sua di San Nastasò,
  Purchè 'l nodrisca, e sazii, ella è madonna.

Chi dirà ciò, nemmen dovria far caso,
  Quand il corpo si generi, e si forme,
  Di che sangue si faccia, ed in che vaso.

Qual ragion vuole, o cosa troppo enorme !
  Che se del sangue vostro entro si pasce,
  Poi fuori abbia alimento sì difforme ?

E che la nobiltà, che seco nasce,
  E 'l chiaro nome, e i bei principj onesti
  Si corrompan col latte nelle fasce ;

But if the pleasing task ye still refuse,

Ah deaf alike to nature and the muse !

Or if the plenteous stream, to you denied,

Must from a richer fountain be supplied ;

Let prudence then th' important choice direct,

Nor let your offspring mourn a new neglect.

—To seek a nurse ye trace the country round,

At length the mercenary aid is found : (k)

Some wretch of vulgar birth and conduct frail ;

Some known offender, flagrant from the jail ;

In mind an ideot, or depraved of life,

A shameless strumpet, or impoverished wife ;

Or be she brown, or black, or fresh, or fair,

Or to the mother no resemblance bear,

She brings, it seems, a full and flowing breast,

—Enough—your care excuses all the rest.

Born of high blood, whose worth no stain defiles,

Say can ye choose a nurse from broad St. Giles ?

Heedless what venom taints the stream she gives,

So your stall'd offspring vegetates and lives. (l)

Why

E 'l petto altrui quasi gli ammorbi, e impesti ?
   Qual è 'l villan sì rozzo, e si ignorante,
   Che in nobil tronco unqua vil ramo innesti ?

Patirem dunque noi, che il nostro infante
   Di sangue gentilissimo formato
   Dentro viscere illustri, e caste, e sante ;

Debba ricever spirto, introdur fiato
   D' un corpo vil, d' un animo cattivo,
   Nell' animo, e nel corpo suo ben nato ?

Meglio saria farlo di vita privo,
   Che in tal guisa il nodrir : poichè si stima
   Peggio assai del morir l' esser mal vivo.

Tanto imprime in un vaso quel, che prima
   Vi si pon, che 'l suo odore indi levarsi
   Non può mai più con acqua, nè con lima.

In questo Ispagna ancor dovrìa lodarsi,
   Ove ogni nobil Donna a mercè tiene,
   De' figli d' una Illustre, Balia farsi.

Anzi in Galizia han ciò cotanto a bene,
   Che senza alcun rossor Donna gentile
   Nati d' altra a sè pari a notrir viene.

Why midst the fellow tenants of the earth
This high respect to ancestry and birth ?
Avails it ought from whom the embryon sprung,
What noble blood sustain'd th' imprison'd young,
If, when the day beam first salutes his eyes,
His earliest wants a stranger breast supplies ?(m)
From different veins a different nurture brings,
Pollutes with streams impure the vital springs ?
'Till every principle of nobler birth,
Unblemish'd honour, and ingenuous worth,
Absorb'd and lost, he falsifies his kind,
A groveling being with a groveling mind.(n)

Th' uncultur'd clown who grafts the generous stem
Ne'er from a worthless branch selects the gem ;
Yet you, with rank and vulgar blood, debase
The genuine honours of a noble race ;
Thro' the young veins the sordid humours pass,
And change by slow degrees the ductile mass.
—Far happier if by early fate opprest,
Your blameless infant seek the realms of rest,

Than

La nobiltà, l' altezza signorile,
  Che tanto da' suoi ceppi oggi traligna,
  Perchè credete, che sia bassa, e vile?

Di che talor la plebe empia, e maligna
  A voi suol recar colpa, e dice, e crede,
  Che al terren vostro indegna pianta alligna.

Questo degenerar, che ognor si vede,
  Sendo voi caste, Donne mie, vi dico
  Che d' altro, che dal latte non procede.

L' altrui latte oscurar fa 'l pregio antico
  Degli Avi illustri, e adulterar le razze;
  E s' infetta talor sangue pudico.

Vediam di sagge Madri figlie pazze,
  E d' onorati Padri infami figli
  Tutto dì per le case, e per le piazze.

Dal latte ogni animal convien che pigli
  Gran qualità, che inchina, se non sforza,
  Che 'l fanciullo alla Balia alfin somigli.

Non pur in quanto al corpo, ed alla scorza,
  Ma su l' animo stesso, e su i costumi
  Il latte, a par del seme, ha quasi forza.

Than prey to pain, dishonour, and disease,
Drag on existence thro' a length of days.

Of kinder heart the matron dames of Spain
The nurse's mercenary trade disdain ;
Proud to supply, in high born worth secure,
The mother's office with a stream as pure.(o)

Sprung from a line of heroes, that of old
Tho' rude were liberal, and tho' gentle bold,
Whose frowns a tyrant's wasteful rage could awe,
Guardians of freedom, bulwarks of the law,
What secret taint, what dread contagion runs
Thro' Britain's noble but degenerate sons ?
—Not on your chastity, ye fair, shall rest
The charge, whate'er th' invidious vulgar jest,
'Tis from his nurse your offspring draws disgrace,
And thence adulterates his generous race.
'Till the kind father sees with wondering eyes
A motley offspring round his table rise ;
Unlike the parent stock from whence they sprung
And various as the breasts on which they hung.(p)

Late,

Così quel vero Sol gli occhi vi allumi
  A seguir l' orme mie, qual io mi sono ;
  E vi toglia dinanzi l' ombre, e i fumi.

Fumi di fasto, ed ombre d' onor sono,
  Ed amor proprio quei, che v' han tenuto
  Tanti anni, e tengon fuor del cammin buono.

Basti, Donne, il mal fatto, e 'l ben perduto ;
  E perdonate, prego, s' io vi pungo
  Con un ago troppo aspro, e troppo acuto.

Ho detto assai, nè pur al mezzo giungo :
  Ma acciochè, Donne mie, non vi dia angoscia
  Più io, che non le Balie, col dir lungo ;
Riposiamoci un poco, e torniam poscia.

FINE DEL PRIMO CAPITOLO.

Late, but not lost, O sun of truth appear,
From error's gloom the female mind to clear!
Shades of false honour, darker mists of pride,
Touch'd by the beam ethereal quick subside.
Self-love his long prescriptive rule foregoes,
And every feature with THE MOTHER glows.
Enough, ye fair, the dread neglect has cost,
The ills experienced, and the pleasures lost;
Yet ah forgive the bard, whose venturous strain
Has dared to give your gentle breasts a pain,
And let him rest awhile, ere yet the song
Vie with the drawlings of the nurse's tongue.

END OF THE FIRST CANTO.

LA BALIA.

CAPITOLO SECONDO.

SE avrò nel mio parlar tanta virtute,
  Che alcuna di voi, Donne, si converta;
  E 'l fero stil da oggi innanzi mute :

Il terrò più, che se mi fosse aperta,
  E spianata la strada di quel monte,
  Ch' io trovai sempre così chiusa, ed erta :

E più che se cingesse la mia fronte
  Quel ramo in guiderdon delle mie rime,
  Che suole ornar chi bee nel sacro fonte,

Cerchi altri nel cantar le lodi prime,
  Ch' io, pur che dal mio dir tal ben proceda,
  Gloria non è, che più gradisca, e stime.

THE NURSE.

IF the rude verse that now detains your ear
Should to one female heart conviction bear;
Recall one gentler mind from fashion's crew,
To give to nature what is nature's due,
—To me, the triumph were of more account,
Than if conducted up th' Aonian mount,
(Long trac'd with anxious steps, but trac'd in vain)
The muse had rank'd me with her favorite train,
Or for my brows had deign'd the wreath to bring,
Worn but by those that haunt her sacred spring,
—Whilst others mount the arduous heights of fame,
To wake your feelings be my nobler aim :

Nor

Ma quando tanto onor non si conceda
  Alla mia bassa Musa, assai mi basta,
  Che del mio buon voler segno si veda.

E se altrui colpa al mio desir contrasta,
  Tempo verrà, che fia tra Donne in pregio
  Non meno l' esser pia, che'l viver casta.

Nè sangue illustre avrà, nè titol regio,
  Che d' obbligo si santo vada escluso,
  E voglia sopra l' altre privilegio.

Così la Parca tanto stame al fuso,
  Donne, de' vostri dì fili, ed attorca,
  Che siate vive a tempo del buon uso.

Se mentre in culla un fanciullin si corca,
  Tanto si attende, o se si facia o scopre,
  Che gamba, o mano, o piè non se gli torca :

E se da poi che fascia più non copre,
  Si batte su le man, qualor le leve,
  Perchè la destra, e non la manca adopre :

Se tanta cura s' ha quand' uom s' alleve,
  In evitar del corpicciuol gli stroppi ;
  Quanto ingegnar la Madre, e più si deve,

Nor yet unblest, if whilst I fail to move,
The fond attempt my kind intention prove.

Ah yet, ye fair, shall come that happier day
When love maternal shall assert her sway,
And crowning every joy of married life,
Join the fond mother to the faithful wife ;
When every female heart her rule shall own,
From the straw cottage to the splendid throne ;
Nor e'er for ought that fortune can bestow,
A mother's sacred privilege forego.
And may the fates, ye fair, your years prolong,
To see accomplish'd all your poet's song.

If, whilst in cradled rest your infant sleeps,
Your watchful eye unceasing vigils keeps
Lest cramping bonds his pliant limbs constrain,
And cause defects that manhood may retain ; (q)
If, when his little hands, from bondage free,
Restless expand in new born liberty,
You teach the child, by reprehension slight,
In preference to the left to use the right ;
—If thus the body claim your constant care,
Shall not the mind your equal caution share

Lest

Che l' alma tenerella non si stroppi
 D' un vizio, o d' altro neo, che seco porti
 Il seno di colei, che sugga, e poppi ?

Vi parrà delle cose a creder forti
 Quel, ch' io vi dissi, o Donne, ed è pur certo,
 Che 'l latte a par del seme quasi importi :

E 'l potrete provar chiaro, ed aperto,
 Se i vostri contemplate, e gli altrui frutti ;
 Come l' intende ogni uom saggio, ed esperto.

Vedrete cinque, o sei fratelli, e tutti
 Di costumi, e di vita assai diversi,
 Come se da più madri sian produtti.

Non fan pianeti prosperi, od avversi,
 Ma il latte, l' alimento lor primiero,
 Che può far buoni gli animi, e perversi.

Or se 'l desìo d' un nespolo, o d' un pero,
 O d'altro, che abbia Donna allor ch' è pregna,
 E troppo si sprofondi in quel pensiero ;

Può tanto, che in quel membro il frutto segna
 Dal fanciullin, che a sè medesma tocca
 La Madre al tempo, che 'l desìo più regna :

Lest early stains, from nutriment impure,
Print deep those blots no future arts can cure?

Perchance the truth your credence scarce will move,
Tho' long experience will the maxim prove,
That what your growing child imbibes when young,
Imports not less than from whose loins he sprung.
—How oft a numerous progeny we find,
Various in worth, in manners and in mind;
Whoe'er the father, we can scarce suppose
From the same mother such an offspring rose.
Yet on the strange event no mystery waits,
Of prosperous planets or of adverse fates,
The plastic streams these qualities instill,
And form the character for good or ill.

If, ere that hour arrive whose awful strife
Gives your new offspring to external life,
Some favorite object, fruit, or flower, inspire
Resistless yearnings of intense desire,
'Tis said that nature's wond'rous power is such,
That on whatever part the mother's touch
Is first impressed, the self same part retains
On the young babe the imitative stains; (r)

And

Quanto più de' poter quel, che per bocca
    Sua propria gli entra, e 'l nutre un anno, o due,
    Latte di rea, di perfida, di sciocca?

E se in uom fermo, e su le forze sue
    La qualità de' cibi molto pote;
    Che può in un, che l' altr' jer prodotto fue?

 ' Usi uom solingo, e pallido le gote
    Quel pomo insano, c' ha 'l color qual negro
    Vedrete se 'l cervello sì gli srote;

Ed al contrario, ancorchè grave, ed ergo,
    Dategli ed oro, e gemme trite a bere;
    Che avrà la mente queta, e 'l volto allegro.

Non pur si può negli uomini vedere
    Quel, che possa ne' parti un' indegn' esca,
    Ma nelle bestie stesse, e nelle fiere.

Provi pastor, come di sen loro esca
    Che la capra e la pecora col petto
    L' una i figli dell' altra allevi, e cresca;

E vedrà riuscir contrario effetto
    Al naturale; perchè il pelo all' agna
    Verrà fuor duro, e morbido al capretto.

And doubt ye, that your infant's earliest food,
Mix'd with his frame, and circling with his blood,
If long imbib'd from some corrupted spring,
Can fail at length its dread effects to bring?
—Even the ripe man, to perfect vigour grown,
Prospers or pines from aliment alone;
Once if he taste the lurid fruit insane,
How throbs his heart, and whirls his madding brain!
Or when with sickness bow'd, with care opprest,
The healing potion sooths his ills to rest.
What then th' effect of food—ye parents say,
On the young babe, the birth of yesterday? (s)

Nor yet alone among the human race
The strong effects of aliment we trace.
—Go, bid the hind employ'd your flocks to keep,
Change but the younglings of the goat and sheep,
The novel food each alter'd fleece will shew,
Soft will the kid's, and harsh the lambkin's grow.
Would you the beagle should his scent retain,
No stranger teat your genuine brood must drain;
Even wolves rapacious half their rage resign,
Fed with the milk-stream from the race canine.

Nor

E i cagnuoli o sian nostri, o di Brettagna,
  Perchè 'l valor de' padri in lor si servi,
  Non den latte assaggiar di strana cagna.

E i lupi esser men ladri, e men protervi
  Col canin latte, ed alterar di pelo
  Vedrà, se a prova un Cacciator l' osservi.

Cangia negli arbor frutti, e fronde, e stelo
  Il trarsi in altra terra la lor sete,
  Svelti da quella, ove pria vider cielo.

Arbor felice verdeggiar vedrete
  Nel seno d' una valle opaca, e molle,
  E far l' aria odorata, e l' ombre liete;

E trapiantata in qualche poggio, o colle,
  Il nudrimento dalla nuova terra
  Ogni vaghezza, ogni splendor le tolle.

Oltre che in altrui danno da voi s' erra,
  Mentre altre son de' vostri parti altrici;
  Voi stesse a voi vi procacciate guerra.

Non dite : o tempi tristi, ed infelici!
  Quando siete dai figli voi neglette;
  O essi son de' padri poco amici:

Nor to the various vegetable tribe
Imports it less what juices they imbibe ;
The vigorous plant in some mild spot that blooms,
Spreads its green shade, and breathes its rich perfumes,
But if to some ungenial soil convey'd,
Soon mourns its fragrance lost, its strength decay'd.(*t*)

Nor feels alone your hapless babe his wrongs ;
To you severer penitence belongs—
Shall modern times your censures keen engage
—A race degenerate, an ungrateful age !
That children scorn a mother's smile, and fly
The kind upbraidings of a father's eye ?
—On you, who caus'd the guilt, recoils the blame;
For thus from heaven th' eternal mandate came,
That manhood should with retribution due,
Avenge the wrongs that helpless childhood knew.

'Twas nature's purpose, that the human race
Should, with the circling lapse of years, increase ;
And well her kind providing cares foresaw
Your dread infringement of her primal law ;
Hence

Perchè'l Rettor del ciel vuole, e permette,
　　Che se or ve li togliete voi dinanzi,
　　Poi grandi essi ne faccian le vendette,

Ben previde Natura molto innanzi
　　Questo error vostro; e perchè non s'annulli
　　Il mondo, ch' ella vuol ch' ognor s' avanzi,

Fe' così ghiotti, e amabili i fanciulli;
　　Li fe' più dolci in quelle età più acerbe,
　　E gli adornò di tanti bei trastulli;

Chè spregiati da voi, Madri superbe,
　　Sia chi gli abbracci, e intanto che gli alleva,
　　Con diletto gli affanni disacerbe.

Tener la Balia dunque non v' aggreva,
　　Donne, incarco che Atlante stancherebbe;
　　E'l Bambin sì, che ognor gran noja leva?

Quando per quello amor, che ai figli debbe,
　　Schifar Donna le Balie non volesse,
　　Fuggirle per suo comodo dovrebbe.

Benchè ponga in non cale ogni interesse,
　　Chi è, che soffrir possa un anno, o dui
　　I cordogli, e le noje, che danno esse?

Hence to the babe she gave endearing wiles,
Resistless blandishments, and artless smiles,
That from your arms, unfeeling mothers, thrown,
Some softer breast the tender pledge might own ;
Fulfil th' important task by you betray'd,
And find the generous labour well repaid.

O past all human tolerance the curse,
The endless torments of a hireling nurse !
If to your children no regard were due,
For your own peace avoid the harpy crew ;
A race rapacious, who with ceaseless strife
Disturb the stream of calm domestic life.
—But wiser you with no such ills contend ;
Far from your sight your helpless young you send,
And to your child, yourselves, your God, unjust,
To others yield th' inalienable trust !
That piercing shriek, from anguish keen that flows,
Disturbs no distant mother's bland repose ;
Those looks, that speak the inmost soul, impart
No kindred feelings to a mother's heart ;
Not her's the prompt and interposing arm
When dangers threaten, or when fears alarm ;

Alike

Se date il vostro figlio in casa altrui,
  Mostrate un disamor tutto in un tempo
  E con Dio, e con gli uomini, e con lui.

Nè vedete, s' egli ha suo dritto a tempo ;
  E del bene, e del mal sapete rado ;
  Ed egli è mal trattato il più del tempo ;

E se non è, mel credo, e persuado.;
  E come amar la Balia il potrà molto,
  Se vede che alla Madre è poco a grado ?

E 'l fanciullo ad amar tutto fia volto
  Colei, che baci, e poppe, e madre chiame :
  Tanto gli è 'l vostro, come ogni altro volto.

Rompete quel dolcissimo legame,
  Che la Madre col figlio d' amor lega ;
  Onde più lui, che gli occhi, e sè stessa ame.

E se pur nol rompete, chi mi nega,
  Che 'l nodo non s' allenti, e che men prema,
  Mentre altra al vostro officio si delega ?

Quel pensier, quel fervor, quell' ansia estrema,
  Che intorno ai figli, o Madri, v' arde, e punge,
  Se son lontani, intepidisce, e scema.

Alike to her whate'er her child sustains,
Its smiles, or tears, its pleasures, or its pains.

But happier fortunes on your babe attend;
His helpless infancy has found a friend.
Leaps his young heart with undissembled bliss
At the fond look, soft smile, or gentle kiss;
Whilst by his lips the milky orbs are prest,
The soft affections spring within his breast;
'Till the pleas'd hireling owns the tender claim,
And to a mother's office joins the name.(u)
But ah, for ever lost the ties that bind
In links of filial love the infant mind;
All that maternal sympathies impart,
Mix'd with each sense, and twin'd around the heart;
The hope that every bliss to rapture swells;
The care that every threatening ill repels;
The smile that mingles with affection's tear,
And speaks the favour'd object doubly dear.
Each soft emotion frigid absence chills,
And love's young transports cold indifference kills,
—Absence, like death, the object long remov'd
Leaves but the memory of what once was lov'd;

Nor

Chi non sa, che ogni oggetto, che sia lunge
   Di vista altrui, se 'l tempo non è corto,
   Dal cor, come dagli occhi, si disgiunge ?

Poco è maggior l' obblio d' un figlio morto
   Di quel d' un vivo, e messo in un villagio
   A pro de' contadini, ed a diporto.

Vien rozzo, e poco generoso, e saggio :
   Quel è 'l villan, che 'l tiene, e la casuccia,
   Tal sarà 'l petto suo, tale il coraggio.

Vi vien la Balia a casa ogni festuccia
   Coi figli, ed altri ; e se non han lor mensa,
   E carezze, e lusinghe, ella si cruccia ;

E se riede a man vota, tiensi offensa ;
   Nè vi vien mai, nè figlio mai vi mostra,
   Che di borsa non scemi, e di dispensa.

Se tenete la Balia in casa vostra,
   Più si pate in quei mesi, che in cento anni ;
   Se tanto può durar la vita nostra,

Oh s' io volessi raccontarvi i danni,
   Che ne apporta il tener d' una Nutrice,
   E i dispetti, e gl' incomodi, e gli affanni,

Nor more severe the hapless infant's lot
Who dies untimely, than who lives forgot.(w)

In idle hours, or when some festal day
Wakes to rude mirth the giddy and the gay,
She brings your infant child—nor yours alone
But all she feeds, another's or her own.—
With smiles and kindness you the flock receive,
Nor whatsoe'er she ask, refuse to give,
Lest whilst she swells with jealousy or rage
Your infant's sufferings should her wrath assuage ;
If in your house you keep the living pest,
Farewell to comfort, and farewell to rest,
For ah, what tongue can tell the care that springs,
The keen vexation such an inmate brings ?
—Yet might I hope, ye fair, nor hope in vain,
My hands could free you from your galling chain,
Could lead to that domestic heaven, which knows
Approving bliss, and well deserv'd repose,
Prompt were my aid.   Nor less the secret ire
That in my bosom heaves with smother'd fire
Calls for th' impassion'd verse.   O may the strain
Promote your peace, whilst it relieves my pain !

Who

Sarebbe, Donne mie, come si dice,
  Un golfo entrar, che non ha fondo, o riva ;
  E vi vorrebbe ingegno più felice.

Ed oltre ch' io ve ne ragioni, o scriva
  Per tor di collo a voi cotesto giogo,
  Che di riposo, e di piacer vi priva ;

Follo anche volentier, perchè mi sfogo,
  Mentre ne parlo altrui, l' ira, e la rabbia,
  Che arder mi fan più che fornace, o rogo.

L' esser ingrata è 'l minor mal, ch' ella abbia,
  Questa schiera, che 'l mondo oggi conturba :
  Ciò che lor fassi, è un gittar seme in sabbia.

Più disagia, e danneggia, e lógra turba
  Ne' tetti altrui l' albergo d' una Balia,
  Che non fan di soldati una gran turba :

Soldati non di Spagna, ma d' Italia,
  E che sian di quei Bruzii, o del paese,
  Che prima salutò la nave Idalia.

Io ho tanto imparato alle mie spese,
  Che predicar potrei cento quaresme
  Dell' esser lor sì strano, e sì scortese ;

Who can the vices of the tribe detect ?
Shameless ingratitude their least defect.
Dispense your bounty with a liberal hand,
'Tis thrown in air, or sown upon the sand.
To greater insults must you daily stoop
Than from th' invasion of a hostile troop.
—Not a gay troop of British volunteers,
Who charm your eyes while they dispel your fears ;
But such as found in Buonaparte's train
Pour their fierce myriads o'er Italia's plain.
But O to paint the torment and the curse
If once your doors admit an hireling nurse,
Were endless waste of paper and of time,
Abuse of patience, and abuse of rhime ;
Nor need I here the irksome story tell ;
From your own sufferings known I fear too well.

Tread as you will, your cautious feet will slide ;
No art can save you, and no prudence guide.
Pleas'd with your child, a fond caress bestow,
—Her pride no equal recompense can know.
Frown—and her breast its milky spring repels,
Or drops with venom as with rage she swells,

Sooth'd

E empirne, non che i fogli, ma le resme:
    Ma perchè il più di voi credo, che n' aggia,
    Vel potrete pensar per voi medesme.

Non è persona così destra, e saggia,
    Che con la Balia sua, tra fosco e chiaro,
    Schermir si sappia, che talor non caggia.

Se mostrate, il fanciullo esservi caro,
    E gradir lei, l' orgoglio più s' infiamma;
    E l' ingordiggia sua non ha ripora.

Se fingete il contrario, la sua mamma
    Trova il bambin asciutta, o d' ira calda:
    Venen, non latte è quel, che sugge, e mamma.

Qual è troppo sfacciata, qual ribalda;
    (Cosa che importa ad onorate case)
    Qual ritrosa, qual ruvida, qual balda.

Bisogna ch' uom più spie, guati, ed annase
    In sceglier Balia, e Santi e Dio c' invochi,
    Che in tor Donna non fa, con cui s' accase.

Che guardi, ond' ella viene, e di quai lochi;
    E ben si può tener avventuroso
    Chi Balia incontri che abbia de' suoi pochi.

Sooth'd by no kindness, by no threats subdued,
Perverse, lascivious, insolent, and rude ;
Ah wretched he whom adverse fates ordain
To choose an inmate from so dire a train,
While scarcely less depends his peace of life
Upon his children's nurse than on his wife.

This can ye bear ? another curse awaits ;
Her tribe of followers then besiege your gates.
Brothers, of doubtful kin, and friends by dozens,
With female troops of sisters, aunts, and cousins ;
Without reproof you hear their loud carouse,
Whilst frighted order abdicates your house.
—Perchance some husband comes to claim his due,
Some sturdy lover lurks amidst the crew,
Then vain your vigilance, in caution's spite,
(Watch'd thro' the day) she cheats your care by night.
Pregnant—her breasts refuse the due supply,
Their source perverted, and their fountains dry.

Sick, pale, and languid, when your infant's moans
Speak its soft sufferings in pathetic tones,

When

Albergar tutto il giorno or frate, or sposo,
  Or altrui, che per frate ella v' additi,
  Non è noja, che turba ogni riposo?

L' intrattenerli, e 'l far lor de' conviti,
  E l' altro saria poco; ma bisogna,
  Che noi guardiam le mogli dai mariti:

Non già che in casa altrui faccian vergogna,
  Ma ch' ella non s' impregni, onde corrotte
  Sian le due fonti, o arida la spogna.

E perchè tutte son voraci, e ghiotte,
  Star vi convien con gli occhi aperti sempre;
  Che se nò 'l dì v' inganneran la notte.

Non par, che 'l sangue, o Donne, vi si stempre,
  Quando il vostro fanciullo infermo piange,
  E la Balia bisogna che si tempre?

Chi temprerà villana sì, che mange
  Quel, che a lui giovi, e schifi quel, che noccia;
  E per due giorni cibo, e vita cange?

Chi impetrerà da lei, che una sol goccia
  Ber voglia d' un liquore, o d' un sciropo?
  E s' una volta il bee, cento il rimproccia.

When nature asks a purer lymph, subdued
By needful physic, and by temperate food,
Say will the nurse her wonted banquet spare,
And for your infant stoop to humbler fare?
Or with her pamper'd appetite at strife
One potion swallow to preserve its life?
—Self her sole object—interest all her trade,
And more perverse the more you want her aid;
Sinks the poor babe without a hand to save,
And from the cradle steps into the grave.

What numbers thus whom length of years had blest,
Untimely fall, by early fate opprest!
Life's cheerful day ere yet enjoy'd, resign'd,
—The dread abuse depopulates mankind.
Nor happier he who doom'd his years to fill,
Drinks with his milk the seeds of future ill;
Born but to weep, and destin'd to sustain
A youth of wretchedness, an age of pain;
Halt, deaf, or blind, to drag his weight of woe,
'Till death in kindness lays the sufferer low.

Once

Quando di lor bontà s' ha maggior uopo,
   Allor son più malvage, e sconoscenti;
   E l' util solo han per bersaglio, e scopo.

Quanti vedete nelle fasce spenti
   Fanciulli, che sarian forse invecchiati,
   Se non bevean quei latti sì nocenti.

Chi potrà tutte dir le infirmitati,
   Che 'l latte improprio nei fanciulli arreca,
   Onde poi grandi, e vecchi son vessati?

Un assorda, un ammuta, un altro accieca,
   Un altro se ne va sempre carpone,
   Finchè la Parca il filo rompe, e seca.

Quanti sono i perigli, ove uom si pone;
   E quel, che è peggio, ov' egli spesso incorre,
   Quando non si conoscan le persone!

Quanti credendo di venire a torre
   Quel ben, che i figli nutre, e sostien vivi,
   Dánno in quel mal, che Francia, e 'l mondo corre!

E 'l povero innocente, pria che arrivi
   All' età del peccar, quei morbi prova,
   Che Dio dà per flagello dei lascivi.

Once exil'd from your breast, and doom'd to bring
His daily nurture from a stranger spring,
Ah who can tell the dangers that await
Your infant ? thus abandon'd to his fate.
Say, is there one with human feeling fraught
Can bear to think, nor sicken at the thought,
That whilst her babe, with unpolluted lips,
As nature asks, the vital fountain sips;
Whilst yet its pure and sainted shrine within
Rests the young mind, unconscious of a sin,
He with his daily nutriment should drain
That dread disease which fires the wanton's vein ;
Sent as the fiercest messenger of God,
O'er lawless love to wave his scorpion rod ? (x)

Strange is the tale, but not more strange than true,
And many a parent may the treachery rue,
Who for their child, neglected and unknown,
Receive a changeling, vainly deem'd their own.
For witness, Ariosto's scenes peruse ; (y)
—Who shall a poet's evidence refuse ?
But say what end the impious fraud secures ?
—Another's child thus takes the place of yours.

                                        Meanwhile

Cosa dirò, che parrà strana, e nuova ;
  E siate certe, o Donne, che ad alcune
  Madri avvenuto esser talor si trova ;

Che i figli vi si cangian nelle cune :
  (Vi parrà la Commedia d' Ariosto.)
  Perchè? direte : per cangiar fortune.

Chè tal, che dalla madre esser esposto
  Doveva alla pietà di chi 'l pigliasse,
  Divien Signor nell' altrui loco posto.

Ed ella, che 'l cangiò, tacita stasse,
  E tra sé gode il ben, che al figlio ha dato ;
  E a tempo, se le par, conoscer fasse.

E colui quando 'l sappia, s' egli è grato,
  Pargli aver alla Madre obbligo doppio ;
  Pria chè 'l fece uomo, e poi chè 'l pose in stato.

Sempre vi trema il cor di qualche stroppio,
  Mentre le Balie in braccio i fanciulli hanno ;
  E vi par d' ora in ora udir lo scoppio.

Si fan peggior le Balie d' anno in anno ;
  Nuove leggi ogni dì sono introdutte,
  E tutte in util loro, e in altrui danno.

Meanwhile, secure the crafty dame can wait
Her ripening project, and enjoy the cheat ;
Reap for her son the fruit of all your toils,
And bid him riot in your children's spoils.
Then, hopeful of reward, no more she hides
Her guilt, but to his secret ear confides ;
Delighted thus a double boon to give,
First life itself, and next the means to live.

What ceaseless dread a mother's breast alarms
Whilst her lov'd offspring fills another's arms !
Fearful of ill she starts at every noise,
And hears, or thinks she hears, her children's cries.
Whilst more imperious grown from day to day,
The greedy nurse demands increase of pay.
Vex'd to the heart with anger and expense,
You hear, nor murmur at her proud pretence ;
Compell'd to bear the wrong with semblance mild,
And sooth the hireling as she sooths your child.
—But not the dainties of Lucullus' feast
Can gratify the nurse's pamper'd taste ;

Nor,

Vonno i gran soldi, von le vesti tutte
   Dei figli vostri ; e s' una lor si vieta,
   Attendete veder le poppe asciutte.

Bisogna ch' uom le tratti da Poeta,
   Sebben vena ei non ha ; chè tutte vonno
   Quella canzon per lor, non per noi lieta.

Per estirpar da noi quantunque ponno,
   Cercan di quelle voci anco esser paghe,
   Che su la cuna cantano : vien, sonno.

Sempre dei nostri danni elle son vaghe :
   Se le deste le cene di Lucullo,
   Non sperate, che Balia se ne appaghe.

Sia pur vezzoso, e vago il bel fanciullo,
   Che più vi dà la Balia angosce, e duoli,
   Ch' ei non vi potrà dar gioja, e trastullo.

Rara è la Balia, che non furi, o involi :
   Vi è forza sempre star sopra di voi,
   Nè mai forzier lasciar aperti, e soli.

Non pur i tempi d' oggi insegnan noi,
   Ma degli antichi molti esempli avemo,
   Che ogni Madre s' allatti i figli suoi.

Finger balia di Romolo, e di Remo
   La lupa, o Donne, che pensate sia,
   Se interpretar la favola vorremo ?

Nor, tho' your babe in infant beauty bright,
Spring to its mother's arms with fond delight,
Can all its gentle blandishments suffice
To compensate the torments that arise
From her to whom its early years you trust,
—Intent on spoil, ungrateful, and unjust.

Were modern truths inadequate to shew
That to your young a sacred debt you owe,
Not hard the task to lengthen out my rhimes
With sage examples drawn from ancient times. (z)
Of Rome's twin founders oft the bard has sung,
For whom the haggard wolf forsook her young :
True emblem she of all th' unnatural crew
Who to another give their offspring's due. (aa)
But say, when at a SAVIOUR's promis'd birth
With secret gladness throb'd the conscious earth,
Whose fostering care his infant wants represt,
Who lav'd his limbs, and hush'd his cares to rest ?
—She, at whose look the proudest queen might hide
Her gilded state, and mourn her humbled pride.

She

Un mostrar, che ciascun' altra che dia,
  Fuorchè la Madre, latte al fanciullino,
  E' lupa ingorda, e fera ladra, e ria.

E s' egli è Istoria, fu voler Divino,
  Che nel fondar di Roma mostrar volse
  Le grandezza de' fati, e del destino.

Chi nudrì, chi lavò, chi in fasce accolse
  Il Re del ciel, la Maestà divina,
  Quand' Uom quì nacque, e carne umana tolse?

Se non la Madre sua, l' alta Reina,
  Quella che fu nel mondo, ed è sol una,
  A cui la terra assorge, e 'l ciel inchina.

Ella sel tenne in grembo, ed Ella in cuna;
  Ella a città portollo, ed Ella a tempio;
  Nè parte mai v' ebbe altra donna alcuna.

Or non dovrìa bastar quest' uno esempio,
  Se avete del devoto, e del fedele,
  A ritrarvi d' error sì crudo, ed empio.

Oh quante son le colpe, e le querele,
  (Parmi quasi d' udirne le parole)
  Che vi si dan d' un atto si crudele!

Natura innanzi a voi di voi si dole,
  Da poi che, mercè vostra, in van si affanna
  Per darvi da nutrir la cara prole.

She all her bosom's sacred stores unlock'd,
His footsteps tended, and his cradle rock'd;
Or, whilst the altar blaz'd with rites divine,
Assiduous led him to the sacred shrine:
And sure th' example will your conduct guide,
If true devotion in your hearts preside.

But whence these sad laments, these mournful sighs,
That all around in solemn breathings rise?
Th' accusing strains in sounds distinct and clear
Wake to the sense of guilt your startled ear.
Hark, in dread accents nature's self complain,
Her precepts slighted, and her bounties vain!(*bb*)
See sacred pity, bending from her skies,
Turns from th' ungenerous deed her dewy eyes.
Maternal fondness gives her tears to flow
In all the deeper energy of woe;
Whilst Christian charity, enshrin'd above,
Whose name is mercy and whose soul is love,
Feels the just hatred that your deeds inspire,
And where she smil'd in kindness burns with ire.

See

Ogni animal, ch' è in terra, vi condanna :
  La Pietà, che dal Cielo il tutto mira,
  Di là, per nò 'l veder, gli occhi s' appanna.

La Carità materna ne sospira ;
  E la Cristiana di ben fare ingorda,
  Quanto arder suol d' amor, tanto arde d' ira.

La Nobiltà dell' altrui macchie lorda,
  Via più ch' altra che sia, par che si lagne ;
  Chè col sangue contrario mal s' accorda.

Valor, e Cortesia seco ne piagne,
  E la Creanza, ed ogni altra virtude,
  Che della Nobiltà sono compagne.

I vostri figli con quel pianto rude,
  Quando fére maggior le orecchie vostre,
  Chiaman voi, Madri, dispietate, e crude.

In somma il vostro error par che ognun mostre ;
  Contra voi gridi 'l ciel, la terra, e 'l mare,
  Il petto, il sangue, le viscere vostre.

Disponetevi omai, Donne mie care,
  Al santo ufficio, ad opra così buona,
  Miglior, di quante ne potreste fare.

E 'n dirvi Donne, intendo ogni persona
  Del nobil sesso ; ed una non ne salvo,
  *Sia quantunque   *   **

See true nobility laments his lot,
Indignant of the foul degrading blot ;
And courtesy and courage o'er him bend,
And all the virtues that his state attend.
But whence that cry that steals upon the sense !
'Tis the low wail of injur'd innocence ;
Accents unform'd, that yet can speak their wrongs
Loud as the pleadings of a hundred tongues.
See in dread witness all creation rise,
The peopled earth, deep seas, and circling skies ;
Whilst conscience with consenting voice within,
Becomes accomplice and avows the sin.

Ah then, by duty led, ye nuptial fair,
Let the sweet office be your constant care.
With peace and health in humblest station blest,
Give to the smiling babe the fostering breast ;(cc)
Nor if by prosperous fortune placed on high,
Think ought superior to the dear employ.
Shall the lov'd burthen that so long ye bore,
Your alter'd kindness from its birth deplore ?

Whilst

Portate tutte i vostri parti, salvo
   Quelle ch' anno il petto arido, o son egre,
   Così or nel grembo, come pria nell' alvo.

Nodritevegli voi ognor più allegre,
   Perchè parte maggior non v' abbia il Padre ;
   Siate de' Figli vostri Madri integre,

Non è pazzia, Giovani mie leggiadre,
   Che nobil Donna potendo esser tutta,
   Mezza si faccia del suo figlio madre ?

Che foggia è questa così scema, e brutta
   Di mezze Madri, e di partito pondo,
   Dal gran nemico su la terra indutta ?

Così fu sempre, mi direte, il mondo :
   Quel che le nostre Madri a noi già denno,
   Or noi rendemo ai figli. Io vi rispondo,

Facendo voi quel, ch' altre pria non fenno,
   Senza che Chiesa il dica, o Re il comandi,
   Maggior sarà la bontà vostra, e 'l senno.

E quanto più sarete illustri, e grandi
   Primiere a poner man, che ai nostri tempi
   Pensier sì santo in opera si mandi ;

Più sarete cagion coi vostri esempi,
   Che d' imitarvi ognuna si diletti,
   Com' ella in voi tanta virtù contempi.

Whilst the fair orbs with healthful nurture swell'd
Throb for the kind relief by you withheld?
Not half a mother she whose pride denies
The streaming beverage to her infant's cries,
Admits another in her rights to share,
And trusts his nurture to a stranger's care ; (*dd*)
But you whose hearts with gentle pity warm,
Pure joys can please and genuine pleasures charm,
Clasp your fair nurselings to your breasts of snow,
And give the sweet salubrious streams to flow,
Let kind affections sway without controul,
And thro' the milk-stream pour the feeling soul.
—What tho' th' inveterate crime, the dire disgrace,
From elder years to modern times we trace,
Nor earthly laws its wasteful rage restrain,
Be yours the task to break the wizard chain ;
So shall the glorious deed your sex inspire,
All earth applaud you, and all heaven admire.

O happier times, to truth and virtue dear.
Roll swiftly on ! O golden days appear !

Or se vedessi (o giorni benedetti !)
  Le Colonne, le Ursine, le Gonsaghe,
  Ed altre tai co' cari figli ai petti ;
Non spereresti, Italia, le tue piaghe
  Veder sane, e tornar l' antica gloria,
  E quelle genti tue d' onor sì vaghe ?
Vedessi la seconda tua Vittoria,
  D' età seconda, ma di fama prima,
  Onde il mio buon Toledo oggi si gloria.
E più per lei sè stesso or pregia, e stima,
  Che per quante vittorie Adria, e Tirreno,
  Affrica, ed Asia, e 'l Mondo gli dier prima.
Vedessi lei nel casto, inclito seno
  Stringer dolce Bambino, e trarne fore
  Nettar celeste, non liquor terreno.
Non ti parria veder Febo, ed Amore
  Poppar sua Madre ; e 'l bel Bambin non latte
  Ivi ber, ma virtù, senno, e valore ?
Donne illustri, e da Dio per norma fatte
  Dell' altre Donne ; la cui luce splende
  Sovra quanto 'l sol fere, e l' onda batte ;
Poichè il riposo, e l' onor nostro pende
  Dai figli (quai si sieno) di voi altre ;
  Se d' allattarli voi vi si contende,
Almeno in cercar Balie siate scaltre.

IL FINE DELLA BALIA.

Of noble birth, when every matron dame,
Shall the high meed of female merit claim ;
Then loveliest, when her babe in native charms
Hangs on her breast or dances in her arms,
Thus late with angel grace along the plain,
Illustrious DEVON led Britannia's train ; (ee)
And whilst by frigid fashion unreprest,
She to chaste transports open'd all her breast,
Joy'd her lov'd babe its playful hands to twine
Round her fair neck, or midst her locks divine,
And from the fount with every grace imbued,
Drank heavenly nectar, not terrestrial food.
—So Venus once, in fragrant bowers above,
Clasp'd to her rosy breast immortal love ;
Transfus'd soft passion thro' his tingling frame,
The nerve of rapture, and the heart of flame.
Yet not with wanton hopes and fond desires,
Her infant's veins the British matron fires ;
But prompts the aim to crown by future worth
The proud preeminence of noble birth.

THE END.

NOTES.

CANTO I.

(a) Whilst yet conceal'd, in life's primæval folds.

MANY of the arguments adduced by Tansillo in the foregoing poem, may be found in the *Noctes Atticæ* of Aulus Gellius, *lib.* xii. *cap* 1. Where that author has inserted a dissertation of the philosopher Favorinus on this subject, in which is the following passage, which the Italian poet has closely followed, " Quod est " enim hoc contra naturam imperfectum atque dimidiatum matris genus, peperis- " se, ac statim ab sese abjecisse ? aluisse in utero, sanguine suo, nescio quid, quod " non videret : non alere nunc suo lacte quod videat, jam viventem, jam hominem, " jam matris officia implorantem ?" That the abuse is of very ancient date is sufficiently evident, as well from this passage as from many others in the Roman authors, but the plea of prescription ought not to be allowed in this case, nor ought a reform to be wholly despaired of ; for certainly *nullum tempus occurrit naturæ*.

(b) Hangs on the lip, or wantons in the cheek.

From Favorinus again, " An tu quoque putas, naturam feminis mammarum " ubera, quasi quosdam nævulos venustiores, non liberorum alendorum, sed or- " nandi pectoris causa dedisse ?"

(c) And with disease contaminate the blood.

That the refusal of a mother to give suck to her child is a deviation from one of the first laws of nature, is clearly evinced by the unfavourable effect this con- duct produces on the health of the mother ; who frequently incurs by this fashionable

onable act of imprudence the risk of her own life, as well as that of her child.
" Sic enim, quod à vobis scilicet abest, pleræque istæ prodigiosæ mulieres fontem
" illum sanctissimum corporis, generis humani educatorem, arefacere et extinguere
" cum periculo quoque aversi corruptique lactis laborant, tamquam pulchritu-
" dinis sibi insignia devenustet."......" On verra" says a celebrated writer on this
subject, " que les femmes qui allaitent elles-mêmes leurs enfans, jouissent de la
" santé la plus parfaite ; tandis que celles qui se dispensent de ce soin, & qui le
" font nourrir par des étrangeres, sont livrées à une foule de maux qui sont tou-
" jours difficiles à guérir, & souvent dangereux pour leur vie."

M. de Puzos.

(d) The kindred guilt that marks this dread offence.

This comparison between the mother who wilfully destroys her child before
its birth, and the mother who wilfully suffers it to perish after its birth, for want
of its proper nutriment, though adopted from Favorinus by Tansillo, is thought
by his Italian editor to stand in need of an apology; he therefore expressly declares,
that his author in this instance must be presumed to have exercised his privilege
as a poet, and to have followed rather the precepts of the heathen philosopher than
the principles of sound morality. The passage in the Italian is perhaps more objec-
tionable than in the translation ; for the author expressly asserts his opinion that
" between the two crimes there is not <i>one ounce of difference.</i>" In the Roman
author it stands thus, " Quod cum sit publica detestatione communique odio
" dignum, in ipsis hominem primordiis, dum fingitur, dum animatur, inter ipsas
" artificis naturæ manus interfectum ire ; quantulum hinc abest, jam perfectum,
" jam genitum, jam filium, proprii atque consueti atque cogniti sanguinis alimo-
" nia privare ?"

(e) And robs her helpless young of half the boon.

That the general plea of inability on the part of the mother to suckle her child,
is in most instances fallacious, may be presumed from the fact adverted to in the
text, namely, that the same nutriment which supports the child before its birth,
is still destined to its use afterwards, tho' differently modified, according to the
difference in the relative situation of the parties ; from which it may be established,
as a general rule (not however without some particular exceptions) that she who
can support a child to its full birth, can also, if she chooses, support it afterwards. Whoever has attentively observed the extreme and almost superabundant

caution

caution of nature apparent in the preservation and increase of both the animal and vegetable creation, will not easily be led to believe, that at this crisis, of all others the most important, she has left her work imperfect.

(ƒ) *Up to the breasts, a living river, sprung.*

" An quia spiritu multo, et calore exalbuit non idem sanguis est nunc in
" uberibus, qui in utero fuit? Nonne hac quoque in re, solertia naturæ evidens
" est? quod postquam sanguis ille opifex in penetralibus suis omne corpus ho-
" minis finxit, adventanti jam partûs tempore, in supernas se partes profert, et ad
" fovenda vitæ, atque lucis rudimenta præsto est, & recens natis notum & famili-
" arem victum offert."

Favorin. ut supr.

(g) *With strength unconquer'd and resistless rage.*

The instinctive affection of brute animals towards their young, is so powerful as to have been frequently employed by the poets in describing the most extreme attachment and fidelity.

" As for his whelps
" The lion stands ; him thro' some forest drear
" Leading his little ones, the hunters meet;
" Fire glimmers in his looks, and down he draws
" His whole brow into frowns, covering his eyes ;
" So, guarding slain Patroclus, Ajax lour'd."

Cowper's Iliad, b. 17.

Ariosto, in his Orlando, *canto* 19, *st.* 7, has the following beautiful comparison.

" Come orsa che l' alpestre cacciatore
" Nella petrosa tana assalit' abbia,
" Stà sopra i figli con incerto core ,
" E freme in suona di pietà e rabbia;
" Ira la invita, e natural furore,
" A spiegar l' unghie, a insanguinar le labbia,
" Amor la intenerisce, e la ritira
" A riguardare i figli in mezzo all' ira."

(h) *Peru*

(b) Peru, or Spain, or either India sends.

It is related by Plutarch, that when Julius Cæsar saw some rich strangers walking through the streets of Rome, fondling and playing with lapdogs and monkeys which they carried with them, he asked, whether their wives did not bear children. But what would Cæsar have thought in our days, says the Italian annotator, if he had seen even a mother, bestow upon the offspring of a brute that fondness and attention which she denies to her own child ? This detestable custom, which outrages nature, and satirizes humanity, is probably more frequent in Italy than in this country ; but is not even here so totally banished, as to render the application of this passage of the poem wholly irrelevant.

(i) No other debt your injur'd offspring knows.

" Facit parentes bonitas, non necessitas."

Says Phædrus in the xv. fable of his 3d book, the whole of which is strikingly apposite to this subject.

(k) At length the mercenary aid is found.

That there are instances in which it is impracticable or improper for the mother to give suck to her child, cannot be denied. By a certain absurd custom, which has often prevailed, and may soon prevail again in this island, the nipple of the female breast is frequently so depressed as to render it throughout life totally unfit for the purpose for which it was by nature intended, and the mother, though enjoying a strong and healthy constitution, and with the sincerest dispositions to perform this first duty to her offspring, finds herself debarred of the pleasure, and perhaps irreparably injured in her health, from the effects of this worse than barbarous fashion. Neither can it be contended, that where the mother is affected by any chronic or hereditary malady, she ought to bring up her child with her own milk ; on the contrary, every effort ought to be made, consistent with the health of the foster-mother, to obliterate by more healthful nutriment, the effects of the original taint. But except in these instances, and perhaps some few others of a similar nature, it may be asserted with confidence, that every mother can and ought to suckle her own offspring. The pretence that a woman is of too delicate a habit to afford sufficient nutriment for a child, is fully refuted by the undeniable fact, that she has already supported it to the time of its birth. " Une femme qui est devenue grosse," says the author

thor above cited, " & qui malgré la delicatesse de son tempérament, a conduit
" sa grosesse à terme, est à plus forte raison en état d' allaiter son enfant ; car il
" faut plus de force pour former un enfant que pour le nourrir." *M. de Puzos.*

(*l*) *So your stall'd offspring vegetates and lives.*

" Sed nihil interest (hoc enim dicitur) dum alatur, & vivat, cujus id lacte fiat."
Favor. ut sup.

(*m*) *His earliest wants a stranger breast supplies.*

" Cur igitur iste qui hoc dicit, si in capessendis naturæ sensibus tam obsurduit,
" non id quoque nihil interesse putat, cujus in corpore, cujusque ex sanguine con-
" cretus homo & coalitus sit." *Favor. ut supr.*

(*n*) *A groveling being with a groveling mind.*

" Quæ (malum !) igitur ratio est, nobilitatem istam nati modo hominis, cor-
" pusque, & animum benigne ingenitis primordiis inchoatum, insitivo, degeneri-
" que alimento lactis alieni corrumpere ? præsertim si ista, quam ad præbendum
" lac tunc adhibebitis, aut serva, aut servilis ; &, ut plerumque solet, externæ at-
" que barbaræ nationis ; si improba, si informis, si impudica, si temulenta est.
" Patiemurne igitur, infantem hunc nostrum pernicioso contagio infici, & spiri-
" tum ducere in animum, atque in corpus suum, ex corpore & animo deterrimo?"
Favor. ut supr.

(*o*) *The mother's office with a stream as pure.*

This custom among the Spanish matrons of assisting each other in the important office of rearing their offspring, is, as we are informed by the annotations of
Ranza, more peculiar to Gallicia, than the other provinces of that country. It
cannot perhaps be denied, that if this duty must be performed by a substitute, it
is a far more agreeable idea to intrust it to a person of character and honour, who
has generosity enough to undertake it gratuitously, that to one whose dispositions
and character are unknown ; but it must also be confessed, that however laudable
the custom may be, there is little hope, in the present state of society, of seeing
it extended to this country, nor perhaps even in that case would it be attended
with all the advantages expected from it. It will be sufficient if our dames of
fashion condescend to perform this duty for themselves, without requiring them
to

to afford their assistance to another. A custom in a great degree similar, and not less commendable, seems to have been established among the Romans, where some matron of distinguished credit and character, devoted herself to the care of an infant family, and to the formation of their minds to habits of modesty and virtue, without however interfering in the office of nutrition, which was wholly performed by the mother herself. Of this character of a nurse a beautiful picture is given in the treatise *De Oratoribus,* attributed by some to Tacitus, and by others to Quintilian. " Jam primum suus cuique filius ex casta parente natus,
" non in cella emtæ Nutricis, sed gremio, ac sinu Matris educabatur ; cujus
" præcipua laus erat tueri domum, & inservire liberis. Eligebatur autem aliqua
" major natu, propinqua, cujus probatis, spectatisque moribus omnis cujuspiam
" familiæ suboles committeretur, coram qua neque dicere fas erat, quod turpe
" dictu, neque facere quod inhonestum factu videretur. Ac non studia modo,
" curasque, sed remissiones etiam, lususque puerorum, sanctitate quadam, ac ve-
" recundia temperabat. Sic Corneliam Gracchorum, sic Aureliam Cæsaris, sic
" Attiam Augusti matrem præfuisse educationibus, ac produxisse principes liberos
" accepimus. Quæ disciplina, ac severitas eo pertinebat, ut sincera, & integra,
" & nullis pravitatibus detorta uniuscujusque natura, toto statim pectore arripe-
" ret artes honestas ; & sive ad rem militarem, sive ad juris scientiam, sive ad
" eloquentiæ studium inclinasset, id solum ageret, id universum hauriret."

(*p*) *And various as the breasts on which they hung.*

" Id hercle ipsum est, quod sæpenumero miramur, quosdam pudicarum mu-
" lierum liberos, parentum suorum neque corporibus neque animis similes exsis-
" tere."   *Favorin. in Gell.*

CANTO II.

(*q*) *And cause defects that manhood may retain.*

As the absurd custom of binding down infants hand and foot with bandages, lest their limbs should shoot out into excrescencies and irregularities, has at length given way to the voice of reason and common sense, so it may yet be hoped, that the custom referred to in the poem, which is neither less unnatural nor less injurious

rious, will in time give way to admonitions frequently repeated, and to the influence of those excellent examples, the number of which is now daily increasing among our fair countrywomen.

(r) *On the young babe the imitative stains.*

The progress of reason and the increasing influence of good sense, have at length nearly banished an opinion formerly very prevalent, and productive of great unhappiness to the female sex, namely, *that the child before its birth is liable to be partially affected by the imagination of the mother.* It cannot indeed be doubted that any circumstance which produces a powerful effect on the mother herself, as sudden fright, apprehension, or distress, will affect the infant of which she is pregnant, and may even occasion its death. But, that peculiar impressions on the mind of the mother during pregnancy, produce external marks on the body of the infant, is an assertion, which after all the pretended proofs that have been alledged in support of it, an attentive inquirer will still be inclined to deny. Not so however the Italian commentator Ranza, who is strongly disposed to countenance the idea, and relates a story of a woman, who after gazing for the first time with great curiosity on an elephant, produced a child with a divided upper lip, from whence appeared a projection resembling an elephant's trunk. That infants are occasionally brought into the world with peculiar defects or singularities is certain; but it is perhaps equally certain, that these singularities would have existed if no such impressions on the imagination had taken place, and that when such circumstance occurs, the mother, unwilling to be supposed to have deviated from the rest of the world without a cause, endeavours in the events of nine months, to recall some one which may be presumed to have occasioned the peculiarity of appearance observable in her offspring. The reasons that might be adduced for this incredulity on a subject which has yet many adherents, are briefly these,

1. The circumstances are not connected together by the usual relation of cause and effect. Every woman in the course of her pregnancy experiences innumerable sensations of surprize, desire, aversion, or dread, and yet no indications of it appear in her offspring. Whilst the incidents to which these deformities are referred, are frequently of the most trivial nature, and such as without having been called to mind by some future circumstance, would have been wholly forgotten.

2. In insanity or lunacy, the imagination is so strongly impressed as to take for reality things the most preposterous, and yet no instances are recorded of children under such circumstances having exhibited peculiar marks.

3. In

3. In the animal as well as vegetable system, there are many circumstances difficult to comprehend, but none that involve a contradiction of the known and established laws of nature ; but a greater contradiction to those laws can scarcely be conceived, than that a mere idea passing through the brain of the mother, should attach itself to some particular part of the child. Nature does not perform miracles ; her operations are consistent.

4. Appearances of this nature on the offspring are not usually resemblances of those objects which the mother may reasonably be supposed to have most ardently desired. If the doctrine were true, we should probably see our offspring marked with other figures than those of cherries and of strawberries ; and should occasionally have to admire the imitative wonders of a gold watch, a diamond necklace, a noble coronet, or a crane-necked coach.

(*s*) *On the young babe the birth of yesterday.*

If this argument be adduced to shew that the child is liable to be affected in its health by the milk of the nurse, as an adult is by the nutriment which he receives, there can be no hesitation in assenting to it, but if, as it appears by the context, the author means to shew that the disposition of the infant's mind is altered by the nature of his nutriment, the examples are not strictly apposite. A man may be relieved by medicine, intoxicated by strong liquors, or injured by poison, but it may not follow from thence, that a child imbibes the disposition of his nurse. A defective argument is however no proof that the proposition which it is intended to support, is untrue. The idea that the nurse imparts to the child dispositions similar to her own, is of very ancient standing, " Nec unquam eos," says Columella, *lib*. vii. *cap*. 12. " quorum genesam volumus indolem conservare, " patiemur alienæ nutricis uberibus educari : quoniam semper, et lac et spiritus " maternus longe magis ingenii atque incrementa corporis auget." The intemperance of Tiberius is upon the same principle ascribed to his nurse by an Italian author.

> " Fu conosciuto quanto il latte può,
> " Nella nutrice, che allattò Tiberio,
> " La qual sempre a' suoi di s' imbriacò:
> " Ond' egli ancor non stetti mai sul serio,
> " Perchè sempre era cotto, e si beeva,
> " Che non Tiberio, detto fu Biberio."

Fagiuoli.

The

The same author attributes the want of affection frequently observable among brothers, to a like cause.

" Da che credete voi, nasca l' amara,
" Discrepanza d' umori, e che s' avverra,
" Che de' fratelli è la concordia rara ?
" Perchè ebber varie balie, ed i pensieri,
" Bevver col latte, lor diversi, e varj ;
" Ond' altri pigri sono, altri son fieri."

(*t*) *Soon mourns its fragrance lost, its strength decay'd.*

" In arboribus etiam & frugibus major plerumque vis, & potestas est ad ea-
" rum indolem vel detrectandam, vel augendam, aquarum atque terrarum, quæ
" alunt, quam ipsius quod jacitur seminis. Ac sæpe videas arborem lætam &
" nitentem in alium locum transpositam, deteriori succo deperiisse."
Favorin. ap. Gell.

(*u*) *And to a mother's office joins the name.*

" Ipsius quoque infantis affectio animi, amoris, consuetudinis, in ea sola unde
" alitur, occupatur ; & proinde (ut in expositis usu venit) matris, quæ genuit,
" neque sensum ullum, neque desiderium cæpit. Ac propterea obliteratis, & a-
" bolitis nativæ pietatis elementis, quicquid ita educati liberi amare patrem, atque
" matrem videntur, magnam fere partem non naturalis ille amor est, sed civilis,
" & opiniabilis."
Favorin. ut sup.

(*w*) *Who dies untimely, than who lives forgot.*

" Et præter hæc autem, quis illud etiam negligere, aspernarique possit, quod
" quæ partus suos deserunt, ablegantque a se se, & aliis nutriendos dedunt, vin-
" culum illud, coagulumque animi, atque amoris, quo parentes cum filiis Natura
" consociat, interscindunt, aut certe quidem diluunt, deteruntque ? Nam ubi in-
" fantis aliorsum dati facta ex oculis amolitio est, vigor ille maternæ flagrantiæ
" sensim, atque paullatim restinguitur, omnisque impatientissimæ sollicitudinis
" strepitus consilescit."
Favorin. ut sup.

(*x*) *O'er lawless love to wave his scorpion rod.*

The resentment shewn by the author against hired nurses, may in many instances

stances be just, but he has totally forgotten to enumerate the injuries and disadvantages which the nurse herself experiences. The first sacrifice which she is required to make, a sacrifice necessary perhaps for her subsistence, is to suppress her maternal feelings, and by discarding her own child, make way for that of another. From that moment all her cares and attention are expected to be transferred to her adopted child, as effectually as if her affections had been changed by a miracle, or an act of parliament. When this point is accomplished, and she can " forget her sucking child," she is then qualified for her office, and has all the trouble and anxiety of a mother without her enjoyments. This employment she is to exercise under the immediate direction and controul of a superior, who, conscious that she has deserted her own duty, weakly endeavours to compensate for the performance of it by an extraordinary degree of fondness for her child, and the nurse (whose affection for it is often much more sincere than that of the mother) is continually harrassed with directions, cautions, and reproofs, that embitter every moment of her life. If her negligence affords a just ground of complaint, her fondness excites a secret jealousy in the breast of the mother, who, whilst she refuses to take those methods which nature has prescribed, to secure the affections of a child, repines when she sees them transferred to another. That the dreadful circumstance to which the author adverts in the text, sometimes happens, cannot be denied ; but it may with confidence be asserted, that it is at least as usual for the nurse to receive infection from the child, as the child from the nurse ; and for this relinquishment of the dearest ties in nature, this abdication of her own humble but peaceful roof, and renunciation of domestic enjoyment ; this certainty of suffering much, and probability of becoming a prey to disorders which may never be eradicated, she is to rest satisfied with a pitiful compensation in money, whilst the dissipated mother pursues her pleasures, and joins in the sentiments of the poet against the pride, the obstinacy, and the extravagance of a hireling nurse.

(*y*) *For witness, Ariosto's scenes peruse.*

I suppositi, a comedy of that author. This circumstance may sometimes happen, says the Italian editor, but perhaps not so frequently as it is suspected. For the parent, observing with disgust, low dispositions and vulgar manners in a child that has been long intrusted to a hired nurse, is apt to conceive that it is impossible such child can be his own. He should however remember, continues the editor, that the manners and disposition of the child are precisely those of the nurse who suckled and caressed him, and instilled into him her own sentiments and habits.

(*z*) *With*

(z) *With sage examples drawn from ancient times.*

It would be strange indeed if the authority of antiquity should be required in support of a practice so essentially necessary to the very existence of the human race, as that of a mother giving suck to her own child ; and it is certainly only as a satire upon his countrywomen, that Tacitus notes this circumstance as a particularity in the manners of the ancient Germans. " Sua quamque mater " uberibus alit, nec ancillis ac nutricibus delegantur." If the reverse of this had been true, and the historian had remarked that women of rank thought themselves degraded if they nursed their own offspring, and such task was therefore delegated to the lowest of the people, it might have been thought extraordinary, and would have nearly rivalled that fashionable practice among the inhabitants of the south sea islands, of exposing their children; a practice much more similar, both in its motives and effects, to that of sending out a child to nurse, than is generally imagined. " An non expositionis genus est, infantulum " tenerum, adhuc a matre rubentem, matrem spirantem, matris opem ea voce " implorantem, quæ movere dicitur et feras, tradere mulieri fortassis nec corpore " salubri, nec moribus integris ; denique cui pluris sit pecuniæ pauxillum, quam " totus infans tuus ?"   *Erasm. in Puerpera.*

(aa) *Who to another give their offspring's due.*

This circumstance is differently explained by Faginoli, who conceives, that Romulus and Remus imbibed their ferocity with the milk that supported them.

        " E per prova si è visto infin, che quegli,
        " Ch' ebbe latte di bestia, fu efficace
        " A farlo bestia diventare anch' egli.
      " Ebbe Romolo, e Remo una vorace
        " Lupa per Balia ; ed ambedue redaro
        " L' inclinazione sua ladra, e rapace."

(bb) *Her precepts slighted, and her bounties vain.*

" Reclamat . . . ipsa natura. Cur terra dicitur omnium parens ? An quod " gignat tantum ? Imo multo magis quod nutriat ea, quæ genuit. Quod aqua " gignit, in aquis educatur. In terra nullum animantis, aut plantæ genus nasci- " tur, quod eadem terra succo suo non alat ; nec est ullum animantis genus, quod " non alat suos fœtus, ululæ, leones, et viperæ educant partus suos ; et homines " suos fœtus abjiciunt ?"

                                                    (cc) **Give**

(cc) Give to the smiling babe the fostering breast.

" Quoties audis puerum tuum vagientem, crede, illum hoc abs te flagitare
" Cum vides in pectore duos istos veluti fonticulos turgidos, ac lacteo liquore
" vel suapte sponte manantes, crede naturam admonere te tui officii.   Ali-
" oqui cum infans jam fari meditabitur, ac blanda balbutie te mammam vocabit,
" qua fronte hoc audies ab eo, cui mammam negâris, & ad conducticiam mam-
" mam relegâris, perinde quasi capræ, aut ovi subjecisses ?   Ubi jam erit fandi
" potens, quid si te pro matre vocet semimatrem ?   Virgam expedies, opinor.
" Atqui vix semimater est quæ recusat alere quod peperit."   *Erasm. ut sup.*

(dd) And trusts his nurture to a stranger's care.

" Oro te (inquit) Mulier, sine eam totam, ac integram esse matrem filii sui.
" Quod est enim hoc contra Naturnum imperfectum, atque dimidiatum matris
" genus . . . ?"   *Favorin. ap Gell.*

(ee) Illustrious DEVON *led Britannia's train.*

That example which the Italian poet could only wish for, this country has experienced, in the conduct of the DUCHESS OF DEVONSHIRE ; who, though
moving in the most elevated sphere of society, with every grace of person, and
every accomplishment of mind, did not conceive that either these, or any other
circumstances attending her high rank, dispensed with the sacred obligation of a
mother to nurse her own offspring.   On the contrary, in defiance of custom, and
in contempt of unfeeling fashion, she persevered in the performance of this in-
dispensable duty, and is said to have found her reward in the great resemblance
in constitution and disposition between the child she nursed and herself.

One such example as this, is a more convincing refutation of all the arguments against this salutary custom, than can be derived either from the imagination of the poet, or the reasonings of the philosopher ; and it will be a lasting re-
proach to the present age, if SUCH AN ILLUSTRIOUS INSTANCE OF MATERNAL
FIDELITY, should fail of producing its full effect, in the promotion of that GREAT
AND RADICAL REFORM in the feelings and manners of domestic life, upon which
the cause of VIRTUE, of TRUTH, and of LIBERTY, and all the BEST INTERESTS
OF HUMAN SOCIETY immediately depend.

THE END.